Katrina gasped when the heat of Skye's body pressed against hers. "You said we had to talk," she said unsteadily.

"I lied." His eyes were fixed on hers in a hard, searching stare. "We've talked, and it hasn't helped. I've taken cold showers, and it hasn't helped."

"Skye—"

He shifted one hand to her face, holding her as if to keep her still, even though she hadn't moved. "I have to know," he muttered almost to himself.

"What?" She was bewildered.

Without answering, he bent his head and fitted his mouth to hers. His hand slid around to the back of her head, long fingers tangling in her hair as he took her mouth with utter confidence.

Katrina wanted to resist, but she was coming apart inside, melting in the stark heat of her need and his. Her fingers dug into the muscles of his back, her body arched in a driven need to be closer, and a primitive wail of desperation knotted in her throat.

It had never been like this before, and she surrendered to it, and to him, because there was no choice left. Her arms tightened around him, and her mouth came wildly alive beneath his.

Skye lifted his head, his eyes blazing with violent emotion. "I knew it. . . ."

WHAT ARE *LOVESWEPT* ROMANCES?

They are stories of true romance and touching emotion. We believe those two very important ingredients are constants in our highly sensual and very believable stories in the *LOVESWEPT* line. Our goal is to give you, the reader, stories of consistently high quality that may sometimes make you laugh, sometimes make you cry, but are always fresh and creative and contain many delightful surprises within their pages.

Most romance fans read an enormous number of books. Those they truly love, they keep. Others may be traded with friends and soon forgotten. We hope that each *LOVESWEPT* romance will be a treasure—a "keeper." We will always try to publish

LOVE STORIES YOU'LL NEVER FORGET
BY AUTHORS YOU'LL ALWAYS REMEMBER

The Editors

THE BOOK TRADER
NEW & USED BOOKS
7829 W. GREENFIELD AVE.   259-1451
3172 SOUTH 27th STREET
6254 N. Port Washington Rd. 645-9666
SELLING & TRADING QUALITY 964-5088
BOOKS SINCE 1980

LOVESWEPT® • 321

Kay Hooper
Aces High

BANTAM BOOKS
TORONTO • NEW YORK • LONDON • SYDNEY • AUCKLAND

ACES HIGH
A Bantam Book / April 1989

If you would be interested in receiving protective vinyl
covers for your Loveswept books, please write to this address
for information:

Loveswept
Bantam Books
P.O. Box 985
Hicksville, NY 11802

ISBN 0-553-21987-1

Published simultaneously in the United States and Canada

PRINTED IN THE UNITED STATES OF AMERICA

O   0 9 8 7 6 5 4 3 2 1

Author's Note

I would like to thank all the readers who wrote to me with comments and suggestions about my "Hagen Strikes Again" series. The level of reader involvement with the series far exceeded anything I've experienced before. Though it was a surprise to me, it was certainly a delightful one. Because of that involvement, several characters and elements present in this final story owe their existence to reader requests.

Some requests, for one reason or another, simply could not be worked into this story; some requests tallied with my own plans; and some requests were an enjoyable challenge. Interestingly enough, in the letters mentioning him, my mail was running almost one hundred percent in favor of a romance for Hagen. That was hardly something I had planned for my semi-comical villain—but I did my best.

I may well do another series one day, and it would have to begin the way this one did—with secondary characters walking onstage and fairly shouting, "Hey, what about *my* story?"

Prologue

The conversation had been going on for some time, and Hagen was beginning to lose what little patience he possessed. Although he gripped the phone with fingers that were tightening slowly, he managed to keep his voice even and calm as he spoke.

"What about Siran?"

"Michael's unavailable." The cool voice at the other end of the line belonged to Daniel Stuart, director of the FBI, and from his tone it was obvious he wasn't in the mood to be helpful. "I've done some restructuring, you know, Chief. Michael's heading my old agency, and he has his hands full."

Hagen found it difficult to contemplate Daniel's recent appointment without gritting his teeth in rage that he himself had been passed over for the directorship. Now he relaxed his jaw and tried to be polite, not his strongest trait. "Congratulate Michael for me. How about one of your bright boys?"

"Sorry. Can't spare any of them."

After counting silently to ten, Hagen said, "You pulled your people off the surveillance I needed a

1

while back and never gave me your reasons for doing so. Is that why I'm having such a hard time now, or am I imagining things?"

Daniel laughed shortly. "I told you why then. I owe those ladies, and I'll be damned if I'll help you snatch Josh Long for one of your devious plots."

"I've altered that plan," Hagen announced.

"Good for you."

This time Hagen counted to twenty. It didn't help much; when he spoke his voice held a definite snap. "I don't give a damn about Long or any of that group. I need one man, Daniel, just one good man."

Daniel's second laugh was one of genuine amusement. "Well, you know, Chief, your reputation's growing. Except for a loyal few that *you've* managed to lose, most of the agents who've worked for you swear they'll never do it again. I'm not sure if they're afraid of getting killed or getting married, but they're quite definite about avoiding you."

Hagen ground his teeth. "I've only lost two agents to marriage: Raven and Kelsey. The rest were one-time volunteers. And Derek, of course, but that wasn't my doing. Sarah still works for me and Michael was always your man."

"Ummm. Still, your name's become synonymous with matchmaking. You've also gotten just a bit too well known for your habit of sending agents into situations with sketchy or deliberately false information. Agents don't care for that, Chief, it makes them nervous."

"Daniel—"

"Look, I don't see your problem." Daniel's voice was sardonic. "Simply draft yourself a few people who haven't heard of you yet. There must be some out there."

Hagen didn't bother to count. He was reluctant to

disclose exactly why he needed an experienced man since he always disliked—and generally avoided—sharing the limelight with anyone, but this time he was driven to it. "Daniel, I have good reason to believe I can finally capture Adrian."

There was a moment of silence, and then Daniel spoke slowly. "You always wanted him, didn't you? Even though terrorists aren't, strictly speaking, your field."

"I mean to get him this time," Hagen said flatly.

"Where?"

"Daniel—"

"You want one of my men?"

Hagen swore. "Gigi's place."

Daniel seemed to consider the matter. "That's a hell of a big place. A lot of people could be hurt. Maybe I should—"

"It's my trap," Hagen told him, "and I'll spring it. I just need one of your men, Daniel."

Daniel argued. In fact, he argued for a good ten minutes, hotly at times. But he finally gave in, saying, "Well, I have one agent who hasn't worked with you yet."

"A good man, Daniel."

"Oh, he's good. He spent some time in Europe, but I've had him on the domestic payroll for a few years now. But you treat him like a pro, Chief, or he'll likely put a bullet in you."

"I don't need a hothead."

"He isn't."

"All right, then." With an effort Hagen kept the triumph out of his voice. "Send him to me."

"He's on his way."

Hagen hung up the special scrambler phone and sat alone in his office, smiling. But he undoubtedly would have lost the pleased expression if he'd been privileged to overhear the conversation going on in a Washington, D.C. office.

"Well? Did he take the bait?"

Daniel leaned back in his chair and grinned at the man sitting in his visitor's chair. "Hook, line, and sinker."

One

The water level was rising, and Skye Prescott wasn't happy about it; he was a bit feline about water and strongly disliked the clammy sensation of wet clothing. Still, he waded out into the man-made lagoon, cursing under his breath. His eyes probed the sparkling water, scanning the blue-tinted fiberglass bottom. In an hour or so this theme park would open for the day, and phony log boats would enter the lagoon after a manic descent down a chute, sheeting water in all directions. He had hoped to avoid the deeper water in the area under the chute, but he realized now he had no choice. Reluctantly he circled closer to the chute, his eyes still fixed on the bottom.

The water was up to his knees, and the bottom was slippery; he had left his running shoes on, and they weren't getting a good purchase on the slick fiberglass bottom. His jeans were soaked above his knees by the time he reached the area near the end of the chute. As far as he could tell, the water was clear, nothing hidden, nothing suspicious. However, he couldn't see beneath the chute; he guessed it was the danger point.

Swearing, he slowly moved toward it. He was suddenly aware of noise as a number of the rides and exhibits in the park were readied for visitors, and that evidence of activity brought a new curse to his lips. If this ride were started up, water pouring out of the chute would make it impossible to search the water at the foot of it.

Skye reached the end of the chute, and just as he bent to his task heard the sounds of water rushing toward him. Instantly he moved back. He wouldn't have been too concerned if his single glance upward hadn't let him know that a large blunt-ended fake-log boat was hurtling down the chute.

He managed, barely, to get out of the way, and as soon as the boat shot into the lagoon began moving toward it with a number of blistering words leaping from his tongue. But the moment he got a clear look at the occupant of the boat he went utterly still, the clash of emotions inside him closing his throat so that no words could escape.

He had forgotten how her long curling hair caught the sunlight in a vibrant explosion of red; he had forgotten that her big eyes, slanted like a cat's, were so unusual a shade of amber and so thickly lashed; he had forgotten that she had high cheekbones that could have earned her a fortune as a model, along with a perfect nose, and a mouth shaped for kisses and dreams.

Skye knew he was lying to himself. He had forgotten nothing. It was just that he hadn't allowed himself to remember.

"Katrina," he whispered.

She was as still as he was, as shocked. Dismay showed in her eyes, and old shadows of pain, and she had gone so white that the three freckles on her nose stood out starkly.

"Skye." Her faintly husky voice was almost without accent. "What . . . what are you doing here?"

He found his voice. "What am *I* doing here? What are *you* doing here? The last time—" He stopped abruptly, then forced himself to continue. "You were in Germany."

She hesitated, then quickly swung her long legs over the side of the lazily floating boat and stood up in the water. Without looking at him she began making her way toward the side of the lagoon. "I work here now," she murmured.

"That's impossible," he said tautly. "Unless—" Again he broke off. *I can't go through that again!* he thought with a savage kind of bitterness. He followed her stiffly and stood facing her when they both reached the pavement. "Who are you working for, Katrina?"

She was silent for a moment, looking up at him—and she didn't have to look up at many men, since she was five ten without shoes. Her slender body was clothed for summer in green shorts and a yellow tank top. She slid her hands into the pockets of her shorts and replied finally, "I'm working for Gigi. Here at the park."

He stared at her, feeling a sudden sick tightness in his chest, conscious of his heart throbbing. Yet despite everything, he knew he still wanted her. Just as he'd wanted her for six long years—and had hated himself for it.

"I've been here for almost five years," she added quietly.

Skye tried to think clearly. How much did she know about Gigi Fargeau, the manager of this theme park? Did she know that the older woman headed a branch of an international intelligence agency that was based here in the southern United States? And did Gigi, shrewd and experienced as she was in the intrigue game, know who and what Katrina really was? Before he could frame any of those questions, Katrina spoke flatly, seemingly reading his mind.

"I defected, Skye. I don't work for them any longer."

"Do you expect me to believe that?" Without his volition the bitterness he had thought long gone flung a taunt at her. "You were good, Katrina, too good to quit. Unless you were running from something. Was that it? Were you slated for punishment because of your failure with me?"

She drew a deep breath, and the amber sheen of her eyes hid her thoughts well. Softly she said, "There was no assignment with you. None. What happened between us—"

"Was a mistake I'll regret for the rest of my life," he told her harshly.

Katrina took a step back from him, almost as if he had struck her, and for a brief moment hot emotion leaped at him out of her eyes. Then she was calm again, but the three freckles on her delicate nose stood out even more clearly. "I know that. You made it perfectly clear before you left Germany." Her voice was steady.

He felt a pang, knowing he had hurt her, and was furious with himself because he cared. He shouldn't care, he reminded himself, he shouldn't give a sweet damn whether he hurt her.

"Ask Gigi. She knows all about me." Katrina sounded tired, and she was gazing at the pavement between them as if she didn't want to look at him.

Skye didn't move. Six years before, the bitter agony of her betrayal had nearly destroyed him; he had been a long time in healing, and he quickly realized that merely seeing her again had reopened those terrible wounds. He wanted to lash out at her now as he had then, to hurt her as she had hurt him. But he was older, wiser, and the professional experience he had gained these last years was nagging at him.

There was something wrong here. Communist agents did not defect to become agents for the other side; but if she was *here*, working for Gigi . . . "Do you work in the park?" he asked abruptly. "Just in the park?"

Katrina lifted her gaze and met his eyes calmly. "I work for Gigi."

"You know what I'm asking."

She nodded. "I know. And I've answered. I work for Gigi."

His thoughts tumbled, clashing together as he tried to make sense of what she'd said. "That isn't possible unless she isn't what she's supposed to be. Or—"

"Or I'm not?" Katrina's smile held the first sign of bitterness he'd seen in her. "If you had listened to me all those years ago, you would have had the answer then. But you didn't. Now that it no longer matters, do you want the answer?"

Skye held his voice steady and made the words blunt. "I'm here to do a job. I have to know if you're a threat."

"That answer is simple. No. Just as I was no threat to you six years ago, not intentionally. You jumped to conclusions, Skye. I understand, and I did in Germany; in our business, survival always depends on being suspicious of everything and everyone." Her voice wavered a bit on the last word, then steadied as she continued. "But you never asked me if what you had discovered was the truth. You believed it instantly. Until then I had thought you trusted me."

"Get to the point," he bit out.

"Very well. You believed I was a communist agent. Not so surprising, they believed it too. They were supposed to believe it. But I was working for the other side, Skye. Your side. I was a double agent."

"Hello, you two!"

Skye turned stiffly to respond to the greeting, feeling curiously numb. He couldn't think, and he didn't dare try. "Gigi," he said in a voice that surprised him because it sounded so normal.

As a child Gigi Fargeau had carried messages for the French Resistance. By her early twenties she had commanded a small but highly effective intelligence-gathering organization operating out of her native Paris. At twenty-six she had married an American military man who had survived Korea but who became one of the first U.S. casualties in Vietnam. After accompanying her husband's body to his homeland, Gigi had chosen to remain in the States.

At a distance of several feet, the petite woman, vibrant with energy, looked twenty years younger than the fifty-eight she cheerfully claimed, but a closer scrutiny revealed that while her face was as smooth as a girl's, her blue eyes were old and wise with experience and loss. She had bronze hair worn short and beautifully kept hands.

"You have met?" she inquired briskly, her sharp gaze moving between the two standing before her.

"Yes," Skye replied, offering nothing else.

One of Gigi's delicate eyebrows rose, and though she was clearly aware of the tension in the air, she chose to ignore it. "Trina, did you check the boats?" she asked, her voice almost without accent after twenty years in America.

Katrina nodded. "They were clean. So is the top of the chute; and all the controls work properly."

"And the lagoon?" Gigi asked Skye.

"Nothing. I'll have to check the entire length of the chute, though. There's no time today, but I'll look at it tomorrow."

A series of loud whistles echoed through the park then, and Katrina turned away from the other two. "The gates open in ten minutes," she said. "I have work to do."

Skye watched her walk away, conscious of his body's response, as if six bitter years hadn't passed and he were back in Germany, watching her and wanting her with a desire that had been powerful and greedy and total. He turned his head finally to discover Gigi looking shrewdly at him.

"She's one of your agents?" he asked in a voice that was strained now because his mind had begun to work again and the conclusions he was reaching were like knives.

Gigi nodded. "My best. Even years ago, when she was little more than a girl, she had a natural talent."

"Years ago?" His mouth was dry.

"In Germany." Gigi's voice was suddenly deliberate, her eyes steady on his. "I recruited her, you see, while she was still in school. She had an unusual maturity, and she had grown up staring at the wall dividing her country. She hated it, hated what it represented. She was more than willing to make the necessary sacrifices. At least until . . ."

Skye waited, staring at her.

Gigi smiled a little sadly. "A young woman of twenty-two may be very mature, yet still bound to follow her heart. Trina fell in love, and had no way of knowing her man was an American agent; he hadn't told her, you see, just as she had kept her own double life a secret from him. It was a tragic thing."

Skye cleared his throat. "Tragic?"

"How could it not be? By the time she discovered what he was, it was too late for her. He had left her, convinced their involvement was only an assignment to her and no doubt horrified himself at having loved a woman who according to all the evidence should have been his enemy. And the KGB, which had believed she was one of theirs, captured her before she could escape. They threw her into an East German prison. It was a year before I could arrange to get her out."

Skye felt his heart stop. "A year?"

Gigi didn't appear to notice his reaction. "Trina couldn't return to West Germany, of course. It was best to bring her here. She is strong, and has put that other life behind her. She smiles now. One day she will laugh. Then that other life will be vanquished."

Skye had forgotten his professional reasons for being at the park, and it was only the second time in his career that he had so lapsed. The first time had been when he had met Katrina. "Where is she?" he asked now, not caring if he were giving himself away.

"When the park is open," Gigi told him, "Trina works in the hotel; she manages it for me."

Without another word Skye turned and headed down one of the paved paths that led to the hotel. He had a map of the park in his head, and knew where he was going.

Gigi gazed after him for a moment. To herself she said, "Almost, I begin to believe in fate. What a strange world this is. So you were the one who left her, Skye. And what now, I wonder. What now?"

Fantasyland was a major theme park in the Southeast, set on hundreds of acres and divided into a number of individual sections dealing with particular fantasy themes. There was the Old West, Seafaring Days, the Space Age, Wonderland—boasting the subheading, For Children of All Ages, and containing characters and exhibits from fairy tales as well as from other well-known stories for children. There was the Circus, other minor sections, and in the center of the park all the traditional rides—roller coasters, the log ride, a huge Ferris wheel, a carousel. . . .

There was a large and beautiful hotel for those visitors wishing to spend more than a day at the park, as well as a golf course, swimming pools, and tennis courts. An outdoor theater provided ample seating for the nightly concerts featuring nationally known singers and groups.

Skye walked past the various sights without a glance, his attention focused on the hotel he was nearing, vaguely aware that the park had opened and that the level of activity had increased sharply as the crowd of visitors began pouring in.

"All right?" a low voice asked suddenly from his left.

Skye halted, but didn't turn. He stood gazing at the hotel, aware that a big man decked out as an antebellum riverboat gambler waited for a response. "No," he answered finally.

The gambler stepped closer, though he remained in the shadows of the decorative shrubbery that lined many of the concrete paths. His wide-brimmed white hat kept most of his face shaded, but beneath a neat black mustache his firm mouth looked a bit grim. "What is it?"

Skye was increasingly conscious of the crowd moving into the area, and felt as well as saw a few curious glances directed at the gambler and himself.

It was dangerous to stand there, and he knew it. But he couldn't walk away from the question. "A ghost out of the past," he told the other man flatly.

There was a moment of silence between them, and then the gambler said, "I can take over. Hagen wouldn't know." His deep voice was very soft.

Skye shook his head. "No. I . . . I think I made a bad mistake in Germany. My information may have been wrong."

Bluntly the gambler asked, "And if it wasn't? Could you go through that again?"

Skye shrugged slightly in a jerky response. "You'd better get to the boat," he told the gambler. "The customers will expect to be dazzled by your cardplay. See you." He walked on without giving the other man a chance to say anything more.

The man dressed as a gambler stood where he was for a few moments, then swore in a low voice and turned away. He was almost to the riverboat that was tied up at a pier in the bend of the man-made river running through the park when a petite blond woman approached him. She was in a costume of the same era as he. Dressed scantily as a chorus dancer, she wore a bright red feather in her up-swept golden hair.

"Garters," she said darkly, taking the arm he offered and beginning to stroll along with him. "You picked this costume out, didn't you?"

"I like them," he replied simply, looking down with some amusement at the frilly garter encircling her shapely leg just above the knee. "Most especially when you wear them."

In a wondering voice she said, "When you told me your life was complicated, I never realized you meant things like this. I don't have to dance, do I?"

"No, you'll sit on my knee while I play cards."

She chuckled, then asked, "Have you seen Skye?"

"Yes."

Alerted by an undertone in his voice, her hand tightened on his arm, and she asked quickly, "What is it?"

"Somebody threw a wild card into the game." He shook his head slightly at her puzzled look. "I don't know much yet. Skye's shut me out—for the moment, at least."

"Has he ever done that before?"

"Once. Years ago." He sighed roughly. "There's nothing I can do about it now. You and I have to assume our places. Ready, love?"

Following his lead, she smiled and said mischievously, "Ready to watch you become a riverboat gambler? Darling, I can hardly wait!"

Smiling, he led her toward the riverboat.

Katrina Keller paused briefly at the desk in the lobby of the hotel to make certain there was no crisis requiring her attention, then went up to her suite on the top floor. Neither Gigi nor the owners of the theme park stinted when it came to the comfort of their employees, so Katrina's rooms were very nice indeed. A corner suite with plenty of windows and bright, comfortable furnishings, it was spacious and lovely.

It was Katrina's home. She had lived there for nearly five years, ever since Gigi had managed to get her out of Germany. Katrina no longer had nightmares about the three-by-five-foot cell in which she'd lived for a year.

She took a quick shower and changed into a pale-gold silk dress that was both businesslike and attractive; since she dealt with guests as a part of her duties as manager, she took care to dress well during her working hours. She always wore her hair up when she was working, and she put it up now in a braided coronet; it was the only style she had found to be neat, since her long, curling hair resisted most efforts to tame it.

Skye had once said—

Katrina canceled the thought instantly, and the face in the mirror never lost its calm expression. One year of her life had taught her the value of control, and it was a lesson the intervening years had done nothing to diminish. Gigi had often called it strength, this ability of Katrina's to focus her thoughts and emotions with total clarity, and Katrina had never offered another explanation to her closest friend.

She could have explained, but she never spoke of that terrible year.

Her mind blank, Katrina slipped her small feet into black pumps and picked up her watch from the dresser, heading toward the living room while she fastened it around her wrist. Three steps into the room she halted, her senses warning her even before she glanced up and saw Skye standing not five feet away.

"We have to talk," he said in a low, hoarse voice.

Her ability to focus and control her thoughts and emotions had never been put to the test in his presence before, but Katrina wasn't surprised to find that ability strained to the limit. Her entire body felt stiff with the effort of keeping calm, and it had never been so difficult to ignore her own emotions. Looking at him brought too many feelings and memories to the surface.

He appeared much the same as she remembered him, but there were differences both subtle and obvious. He was still strikingly handsome, but his face was leaner and harder, his brilliant violet eyes revealing recklessness that had not been so visible six years before. Always a physically powerful man, the years had added even more strength to his frame so that his shoulders were broader now, and beneath the black T-shirt he wore she could see hard muscles.

He had told her he was a twin, that his brother Dane was identical, but she had always found it hard to believe there could be another man like Skye.

Katrina tore her gaze away from him and glanced toward the door, which she had locked behind her when she'd come in. "Still good with locks, I see," she said, her voice calm.

"Katrina—"

She looked at him, keeping her mind blank, shutting the violent emotions away in dark rooms, where they couldn't harm her. "I'm on duty," she told him. "I must go downstairs."

"Not yet. Please, Katrina."

She had never heard him say please before, not like that, and the effect on her was shocking. The outward control held, but she could feel a change within her, as if something she had thought to be dead suddenly woke from a deep sleep and began stirring restlessly. Without immediately speaking, she turned and went to one of the wide windows, gazing through the glass and down onto the colorful park.

"I knew Hagen was sending an agent," she said finally, relieved to hear her voice emerge steadily. "Gigi told me all about it. Does Hagen indeed believe that this international terrorist, this Adrian, will make an attempt on the governor's life when he comes here in two weeks?"

"He believes it." Skye's voice was closer now, almost beside her. "Katrina—"

"If my presence here is offensive to you, I can arrange to go away until it's over. Or I can remain in the hotel—"

"Stop it," he ordered roughly.

She was silent.

Skye drew an audible breath. "I can't go back and change what happened," he said. "But if I made a mistake about you, if the information I received was wrong . . ."

"If," she said in a soft tone. "Such a small word to have so large a meaning. You could never again look at me or speak to me without that word between us."

"What was I supposed to believe?" he demanded. "My God, Katrina, the station chief in Hamburg hit the roof when he found out what I'd done! He couldn't wait to tell me you'd been marked as a communist agent for months, and that my own loyalty was highly doubtful after I'd—"

"Married me," she finished quietly. Before he could respond, she added in the same tone, "The station chief you speak of was Mueller, and since I didn't work for him, he couldn't possibly have known what I really was." She turned suddenly to face him, smiling wryly at him. "But of course I might have known who he was even if I had been completely on the other side. We both know that. Just as we both know there is no proof I can offer you that I was not what you believed."

"I didn't want to believe it." He was staring down at her, his brilliant eyes glittering, and when he went on, his voice had thickened. "I left Germany in pieces, Katrina, so torn up inside I thought I'd die from the pain. I couldn't face anyone, not even my brother. If he hadn't tracked me down a couple of months later, I probably would have managed to get myself killed. God knows I was trying hard enough." He laughed, a strange, rough sound. "That was when I went back for you."

She had gone a little pale, and found it difficult to speak through the sudden tightness of her throat. "You—you returned to Germany?" And when he nodded, she whispered, "Why?"

There was a long moment of tense silence, neither of them moving, the two-foot space between them containing an almost visible barrier they seemed unable to cross. Then, harshly, Skye answered her.

"Because I had to know. I didn't want to believe it, and I couldn't live with the doubt. I told myself you'd still be there in the apartment, that it was all some horrible mistake. I would have believed anything you told me, then. I meant to get you out of the country, bring you back here. But you weren't there, nothing was there except covered furniture and bare walls. And Mueller told me you'd left in the night; he had evidence you'd gone through the checkpoints and into East Germany."

Katrina drew a breath, vaguely aware that her control was slipping further still. He had gone back for her? She tried to keep her voice steady. "I had gone, but not willingly. I should have known they would come for me. I—I wasn't thinking very clearly."

He hesitated, then said, "Gigi told me you were imprisoned."

Katrina nodded, but she didn't want to talk about that, not then, not to him. "Yes. I didn't know until Gigi's friends got me out that you—"

"That I had divorced you?" His voice was still harsh.

She nodded again, and another silence fell between them. It was Katrina who broke it finally, turning a blind gaze back to the window and speaking softly.

"You were right—neither of us can go back and change anything. We both forgot for a while that we had been trained to mistrust and disbelieve. We both forgot what we were. What happened between us *was* a mistake, and how can either of us blame the other?"

"Do you blame me, Katrina?"

She felt tension creep into her, felt a rising heat that was achingly familiar despite all the years that had passed since she'd last felt it. *No. I can't go through it again!*

"Do you?" he demanded again.

"No," she answered finally, refusing to look at him. "I did for a while, of course. But I had a great deal of time to think, and I began to understand what you must have felt. To believe your wife was an enemy agent . . . At least I had the consolation of knowing we were both on the same side."

"Was it a consolation?"

Katrina thought of those endless hours spent staring at four gray walls, even when her eyes had been closed, terror and anguish threatening her very sanity. She tried to push the memories away, but this time they clung stubbornly, and she couldn't find an answer for him.

"Katrina . . ."

"I must go to my office. I have work to do—"

He touched her for the first time, his hands reaching out to grasp her shoulders and turn her toward him. And the strength in those hands was something she had never been able to resist, even though he had never been anything but gentle with her. She kept her arms folded stiffly beneath her breasts and fixed her eyes on the pulse throbbing beneath the tanned flesh of his throat.

"Was it a consolation, Katrina? Tell me." And when

she remained silent, he shook her slightly, his hands tightening on her shoulders.

"No," she answered finally, hearing the strain in her voice.

"Look at me."

She was trying desperately to focus her mind and emotions, wary of meeting his gaze. She had long ago given up any hope of ever seeing him again, and so had not prepared herself for this attack by her memories and senses. "Let me go, Skye. I must—"

One of his hands left her shoulder to turn her face up, his thumb under her jaw and his long fingers warm and hard against her neck. "I said look at me!"

Katrina blinked and almost flinched at the violence she heard in his voice, but forced herself to meet his intense eyes.

"Do you hate me?" he demanded.

The question surprised her, and she answered honestly. "I don't know. I felt so much—and then so little. I don't know." She tried to think clearly. "It doesn't matter now."

"Yes, it does."

Her strongest emotion at that moment was bewilderment. What did he mean? He still doubted that she had been a double agent; she knew that because he had made no secret of it. Though both of them had forgotten their training six years ago, she was certain he, like herself, had never forgotten it since. There could never again be an easy trust and lack of suspicion in either of their minds—and most certainly not between them.

"I don't understand you," she said at last.

There was an odd, twisted smile curving his lips, and his eyes were hard and bright and reckless. "I did everything I could to forget you," he told her, his voice curiously distant. "Everything. But nothing worked, and I hated myself for it. You've been my own personal demon for six years, Katrina, locked inside me too deeply to be torn out."

"I'm sorry," she whispered, her body going both hot and cold at the contrast of the loverlike words and his remote voice. She felt suddenly just a little afraid of him.

"Sorry isn't good enough."

Katrina bit her lip and saw his gaze drop to fix on the unconscious gesture, and panic swept over her. Revenge? Was that what he wanted? She drew a breath and tried to speak evenly. "I know you hate me, but I can't change that."

"Hate you?" He seemed to consider the words as he looked from her mouth to her eyes, his containing the same hard glitter. His lips curved again in a mocking smile. "Hate's a tame word for what I'm feeling, Trina."

The shortened version of her name used only by him and Gigi did nothing to reassure her. She tried to pull away, but his powerful arm was suddenly around her, his other hand still holding her face tilted up. She found herself held tightly against his taut body, and even though she managed to get her hands up to his hard chest she couldn't force him away.

"Don't! Skye—"

He ignored the desperate protest. "We had only a few weeks together. Maybe that's why I couldn't forget you." His eyes were heavy-lidded now, the glitter half hidden. "I have to know."

Katrina forced herself to be still, all too aware that her senses remembered him and were responding to him despite everything. Her body ached with a sudden wild need, and her heart ached with an even more damaging kind of pain. She had hurt him badly six years before, and it didn't seem to matter to him that she had known no more of his secret life than he had known of hers, that neither of them had been honest; now he wanted revenge.

"Don't do this," she said unsteadily.

"I have to. We were always so good in bed, weren't we, Trina? From the very first night. It was storming that night, do you remember? And it was past dawn when we finally slept."

She remembered. She remembered heat and tenderness and a hunger in them both that had refused to be sated. A hunger she could feel rising inside her now, even stronger than before. She had thought those powerful feelings had been lost to her forever once he had left her, and the realization that they had only lain dormant until now was bittersweet, because his voice was hard and remote.

Skye didn't appear to notice her silence. He moved against her subtly, and her gasp made his smile turn satisfied and utterly male. "I thought so. It isn't dead between us. And it must be the demon I can't get rid of. Because I can't possibly still love you, can I, my sweet Trina?"

His head bent so suddenly that she had no chance of evading him, even if she could have escaped the firm grasp of his hand. And at the first demanding touch of his lips, she felt something give way inside her with a violence that sent a shudder through her body, a dam-burst of sensations and emotions battering her from within. All her hard-won control vanished, she was twenty-two again and in love beyond all reason.

Both his arms were around her now, locking her body to his, and his mouth was hard and rough. She shut out the sight of his handsome, implacable face, accepting his driven passion and returning it because she couldn't do anything else. She remembered a storm, and a tender, passionate man who had loved her.

Skye lifted his head at last, his eyes violent for a moment before they were shuttered closed. "All the ifs don't seem to matter, do they, sweet? I can still make you want me."

Katrina couldn't have spoken if her life had depended on it; she could only stare up at him mutely.

He laughed and suddenly released her, stepping back. His face seemed a bit pale, but the mocking smile remained to taunt her. "Still don't know if you hate me?"

She found her voice at last, though it was little more than a whisper. "Don't do this."

"Why not, sweet? You want me. I'll be back when your shift ends. And don't bother running away. I'd only find you."

Katrina was barely aware of the door closing behind him. She stood staring blindly at the spot where he had been, her body still hot and throbbing, her mind numb. And the sound of her own voice in the silent room startled her.

"I won't let you destroy me. I won't."

He had to put out a hand to the wall to steady himself once as he went down the hall to the elevator. It should have surprised him, but didn't. He felt dizzy and sick. He couldn't quite catch his breath, as if he'd run some dreadful marathon. There was an awful pressure in his chest. The instant the elevator doors slid quietly shut, Skye leaned against the wall and thrust shaking hands into his pockets, staring at the indicator that told him he was descending.

"Oh, God," he whispered raggedly.

Across the park aboard a fully detailed riverboat, the gambler looked up from his cards, the tranquility of his expression vanishing for a brief moment as he went pale. Neither his fellow gamblers nor the crowd of fascinated visitors noticed, but the blond sitting demurely on the arm of his chair saw it.

She said nothing, partly because of the crowd around them and partly because she knew what was wrong. It was, he'd told her wryly, both the curse and blessing of identical twins, at least where he and his brother were concerned.

Skye was in trouble.

But not, she realized, in *danger*, because the gambler's handsome face almost instantly regained its tranquil control, and his free hand lifted hers to his lips briefly as he smiled up at her. She accepted the reassurance and tried to be patient until he could tell her what was going on.

Two

"Balloons, sir? Balloons for your children?"

Affronted, Hagen barely paused in his quick stride to send the happy clown a cold glare. And even though the clown's wide smile was painted on so brightly that she could hardly help but look delighted no matter what, her startled wince was visible.

"Sorry, sir!" She retreated hastily, and stood holding her balloons and watching the man stride on while admitting to herself he didn't look the sort of man to have children, much less buy balloons. He had a great leonine head with a cherub's face, a decidedly portly figure confined by a badly fitting three-piece suit, and wore both wing-tip shoes and a fedora that had seen better days. A seemingly comical man, but there had been nothing comical in his frosty glare.

A second clown, this one tall with a woebegone expression painted on his lean face, appeared suddenly beside the happy clown and spoke dispassionately. "You'd throw dynamite on a bonfire, darling."

A rich chuckle escaped the happy clown. "I thought I might as well put it to the test. He's early."

"Yes, we'd better alert the others. Good thing we decided to play our roles from the start. And we should find out from Gigi if he means to stay here for two weeks."

The happy clown looked up at her companion with a smile that wasn't painted on. "Regretting the costume so soon?"

"No." He glanced up as a group of children hurried toward them, his rather hard blue eyes taking on a rare uncertain expression. "I suppose it's practice of a kind."

She giggled and turned toward the approaching children. "A very odd kind."

"Don't laugh at me!" he ordered, sounding both harassed and amused.

She threw him a laughing, tender glance over her shoulder, violet eyes bright, then turned her attention to the children clamoring for balloons.

The woebegone clown stood watching her, a smile playing about his firm lips. He had protested the costume, of course, and had very much enjoyed being persuaded by her to accept it. Still, he was conscious of the absurdity; neither of them fit their assigned roles. Several of the others did, though. But she had been right in believing that Hagen stood a greater chance of recognizing the two of them unless they were totally out of character.

Hence the clown suits.

He would have borne a great deal for her sake; this was certainly little enough. And he had his own ax to grind, of course, since he strongly disliked Hagen's Byzantine hand thrusting into his life without so much as a by-your-leave.

"You didn't practice," she observed severely when the children, balloons in hand, raced off.

"I didn't want you to laugh at me," he retorted.

She smiled up at him, the merry smile he had instantly fallen in love with. "I wouldn't. You're going to make a wonderful father, darling."

His blue eyes softened amazingly as they rested on her face. "I love you, you know," he said.

Some moments later a small, childish voice said indignantly, "Clowns don't *kiss*! And you've let go of the balloons!"

"I am a great man," Hagen said simply.

Gigi, who was the sole audience to this grand statement, accepted it with a solemnity belied by the laughter that had leaped quickly to her eyes. "Oh, of course. I have often said so."

Comfortably seated on the couch in the living room of her suite, he sent her an approving look. But his voice was a bit dry when he said, "No, you haven't, my dear."

"Well, not *often*, perhaps," she admitted, still solemn. "But I do recognize it, I promise you. It is very obvious to me. You're like Charlemagne." She paused for reflection, then added musingly, "Or Hitler."

He ignored that. Splendidly. "Has Prescott discovered anything yet?"

"He hadn't this morning," she replied. "I haven't seen him in hours, however. Hagen, why are you here now? The governor isn't due to come for two weeks."

"Why, I wanted to see you, my dear."

She eyed him with a great deal of understanding and not a little annoyance. "You may have none of my agents," she said.

Hagen looked innocent. "My dear Gigi—"

"None!"

He wore the expression of a man sadly misunderstood. "I hadn't seen you in months, and—"

"You saw me two weeks ago in New York," she said tartly, even more annoyed by this base attempt to disarm her.

"Well, but that was business, my dear."

"Had you something other than business in mind for this trip?" Her voice was wonderfully polite.

He began to look a bit uneasy. "Gigi, if you're still angry with me because of that little argument of ours—"

"Little argument? *Little* argument?"

Hagen cleared his throat but said strongly, "We're both of us past the age for these stupid quarrels, my dear."

In an unyielding tone she said, "Your bags have been taken to the suite at the end of the hall. I have much to do; was there anything further you wished to discuss with me?"

"Gigi!" He saw that her expression was as fierce as her voice had been, and realized somewhat unhappily that she hadn't changed her mind. He had thought she would have by now; in fact, he had been sure of it. But she was a difficult woman, and in twenty years of knowing her he hadn't managed a single time to sway her once she had made up her mind.

She was his only personal failure. She laughed at him and mocked him and more than once in the past had grossly deceived him in matters of business. She went her own way with a fine disregard for his advice or wishes, and he uneasily suspected she always would.

"Good afternoon, Hagen," she said coolly, and rose

to go over and seat herself behind the big desk by the window. Without another word or glance she became absorbed in paperwork.

Finding himself ignored—which wasn't an experience he was at all familiar with—Hagen heaved himself up from the couch and went gloomily toward the door. "Dinner?" he asked with a hopeful expression that would have been effective if he'd looked more like a spaniel and less like a sulky Henry VIII.

She didn't look up. "You'll find a menu in your suite."

He snorted and left, slamming the door.

Gigi's lips twitched.

Katrina didn't run away. Given a choice, at least during the early part of the day, she might have run, but it happened that she was to meet a man for dinner that night. He was an agent, and the information he was to give her was too important to be missed. Since Katrina served as a conduit to Gigi, she could hardly escape the responsibility.

It wasn't only that, however, which kept Katrina at the hotel and made her endure the passing hours with a surface appearance, at least, of her normal calm. Her instant recognition of the very real power Skye had over her had hardened somewhat as she had thought about the situation. She was too honest with herself to pretend she could fight him once she was in his arms, but the twenty-two-year-old girl who had loved so heedlessly had become a woman who had learned to survive, and that hard-won ability was not one she would willingly give up.

He had told her that he had left Germany in pieces; she had said little about her own torment. But Katrina would fight him with every weapon she could find to avoid the pain he had left her with before. She both understood his actions when he had left her so abruptly in Germany and had long ago forgiven him for them, but that was something she had no intention of making clear to him.

He was a different man now, just as she was a different woman, and she thought that this man would turn any knowledge about her suffering into a weapon. It was obvious he was out for revenge now, or at the very least determined to purge himself of the desire he still felt for her.

But it wasn't in Katrina, innately proud and too aware of both the fragile peace she had found and the wild emotions he could still make her feel, to submit tamely to any man. In her was the certainty that he could seduce reason, that she would not be able to fight him physically, and that she would fight him on every other level.

And so she spent the day in her usual calm way, while her mind worked with the sharpness of desperation behind her tranquil expression. Refusing to accept either the full blame for what had happened to them or his implicit demands, she reached deeply into herself to tap the core of implacable determination that had been born inside a cell in East Germany.

"Trina, do you have the guest list?"

She looked up from paperwork she was going over automatically, and immediately picked up a computer printout at her elbow. "Here it is, Gigi."

Her friend leaned a hip against the desk and began scanning the printout, saying dryly, "Hagen has arrived, and I wanted to check the list before it occurred to him to do so. Ah, good! They are all on the sixth floor, then?"

Katrina nodded. "And all under assumed names.

They'll take the freight elevator up and down so as to avoid the lobby." She studied her friend curiously. "Why is Hagen early?"

With a grimace that was both amused and exasperated, Gigi replied, "He wants to mend fences."

"Between you two?" Katrina asked, aware of a long and decidedly stormy relationship that few others knew about.

"Yes." Her fine eyes sparkled in sudden temper. "Do you know that when he arrived he left word at the desk to send his bags up to my suite when they arrived? Fortunately I had the forethought to leave other instructions. *That man.*"

Katrina fought back a smile. Both fascinated and appalled by Hagen—a common reaction, Gigi had told her—she had observed the relationship between him and Gigi these last years with something like wonder. In one sense it was heartening to watch so many tempestuous emotions flourishing between a man and woman who were both fast approaching sixty; in another sense, with two such contrasting personalities it was a small miracle that one of them hadn't killed the other by now.

"He's assuming too much?" Katrina said.

The sound that escaped Gigi might have been a snort in anyone less ladylike in appearance. "Entirely too much. If he thinks he can manipulate me now as he does everyone else he encounters, he will soon learn his mistake!" She reflected for a moment, then added in a much calmer tone and very dryly, "He won't, however. The wretched man has a blind spot where people are concerned, particularly women."

"Why—" Katrina broke off abruptly.

Gigi grinned, and answered the question her young friend had so obviously decided was a nosy one.

"Well, you must admit he isn't *boring*. If I don't kill him, I may marry him."

Katrina blinked and looked at Gigi somewhat warily. In a mild tone she said, "Don't do anything rash."

Handing the printout back across the desk, Gigi laughed softly, "Child, I made up my mind about him twenty years ago."

Katrina didn't know what to make of that, and decided to change the subject. "Do you have a message for Matt? I'm meeting him for dinner in a couple of hours."

"No, no message." Gigi eyed her for a moment, then asked calmly. "Does Skye know?"

"Know what?" Katrina was concentrating blindly on the papers lying before her on the desk.

"That you are having dinner with Matthew?"

After a moment, fully aware that Gigi had no compunction about asking nosy questions, Katrina sighed and leaned back in her chair. Lifting her gaze to that grave face, she said, "Not unless you tell him about it."

"Shall I?"

Katrina hesitated, but she was too good an agent to take the chance of ruining an important rendezvous. "Perhaps you'd better." She managed a small laugh.

Gigi wasn't deceived, and said quietly, "He is the man from Germany."

"Yes." She had never found it easy to confide in anyone, even her best friend, so her response stopped with that.

With a searching look Gigi murmured, "Already he has changed you, *chérie*. There is a look in your eyes I have never seen before. This will be painful for you."

Katrina shrugged slightly and felt her lips curve in a smile. She wondered what her expression looked like to make Gigi's gaze even more intent. "I'll survive it," she said flatly.

After a moment Gigi straightened from the desk, her face troubled. "It is never wise to interfere. But if you need me, Trina . . ."

"Yes. Thank you, Gigi."

"I will warn Skye about your meeting with Matthew." She left the office without saying anything more.

Katrina worked steadily for another hour until one of the assistant managers came on duty for the second shift. Then she went up and got ready for dinner.

"Dance with me."

Katrina halted to face the tall man standing squarely before her, a man who looked almost unbearably handsome in a stark black dinner jacket. His face was masklike, his eyes so completely veiled that she could read nothing in them. His command was an abrupt one, but she had the odd feeling he hadn't meant it to be.

Matthew had gone almost an hour before; she had been summoned to deal with a minor crisis in the kitchen, and was only now making her way from one of the hotel's fine restaurants.

This one, unfortunately for her peace of mind, provided music and a dance floor.

When she didn't answer, Skye took her hand and led her toward the cleared space where several other couples swayed together in time to the slow, romantic music. Katrina didn't resist, nor did she avoid his shuttered gaze when he took her into his arms and held her far too close.

For several minutes they danced without speaking. Then, in that same taut voice, he said, "So silent?"

"Did you expect a scene?" she returned, her own voice as cold as she could make it.

"No, I suppose not." His laugh was hardly a breath of sound. "You haven't changed."

Katrina felt uncertain, and searched his face with an unconscious intensity. He was different, she realized, and she mistrusted the change in him because it seemed so sudden. He had left her only hours before, his implicit demands and remote voice ringing in her ears, having as good as told her they would be lovers again; yet now he was guarded, and she could feel his strain.

"Haven't I?" she managed to say at last.

"You were always so reserved, so calm. I never knew how much you felt."

"You knew," she said before she could stop herself, and wished she had left the words unsaid.

His face tightened. "No. You were loving. Passionate. But always elusive."

Wondering what he could mean, Katrina was silent, unable to say anything between her surprise and the uneasy suspicion of his motives.

"The way you are now," he said abruptly. "Is this going to be your defense, Trina?"

She couldn't misunderstand that. "I'm afraid you're jumping to conclusions—again," she said deliberately. "I'm defending nothing." She thought that he might have winced, but if he did, the expression was so fleeting she couldn't be sure.

His arms tightened around her, and with the fluid grace that was so compelling about him, he began turning the dance into a subtle seduction. His body was hard against hers, his movements so sensuous that her own body responded immediately.

"No?" he muttered.

The sound of the music receded as she felt heat flow through her, and her own heartbeat sounded like a drum in her ears. Only her knowledge of his motives enabled her to keep her expression placid. Her body was his for the taking, and she knew it, but there was more bitter than sweet in that certainty.

"No." She met his gaze steadily, unaware of the clear honesty in the direct look. "If you mean to hurt me this way, I can't fight you. We both know it. But I won't let you destroy me. Not this time."

"Could I hurt you?" he asked roughly.

Katrina didn't hesitate. "Passion without love is always hurtful."

He was staring down at her, a muscle jerking in his lean jaw, and his eyes intense. He glanced around as if suddenly aware of where they were, then swore beneath his breath and led her swiftly from the restaurant. Alone with her in the elevator, he held her hand tightly and said in a grim voice, "You seem to bring out the worst in me."

She stole a glance up at his profile and felt a strange tremor within her. There was something in his face she'd never seen before, something she was almost afraid to try to define. She could almost have believed . . . But it wasn't possible, there was too much bitterness and pain between them; it was only revenge he wanted.

He didn't take her to her suite but to his own room on the eighth floor, and when the door had closed behind them he released her hand and went to the window, standing with his back to her. "You believe I want to hurt you," he said finally in that same bleak tone.

Katrina could have left, but something in the stiffness of his body or the dullness of his voice held her motionless by the door. "You told me—" She broke off as he made a curiously uncontrolled gesture with one hand.

"I know what I told you." He turned suddenly but didn't move from the window. "I said some of the things I've wanted to say to you for six endless years, and it almost killed me."

She swallowed hard. "I don't understand." Was he only toying with her now, attacking from a different direction? She gazed at his white face—and couldn't believe the answer was yes.

He seemed to hesitate, then said steadily, "Can we start over, Trina? Or have I made you hate me?"

Katrina felt oddly suspended; she had nerved herself for a battle, all her will bent on surviving intact, and now she didn't know what emotions were churning inside her. "What do you want from me?" she asked finally, huskily.

"Another chance."

"Why?"

Skye drew a deep breath. "Because I've never been able to forget you. Even when I wanted to. Because you still feel something for me, even if it's only desire. And because we both have to settle with the past."

Her legs felt shaky, and she moved to sit in a chair near the foot of the bed. "No," she heard herself saying.

Skye came toward her slowly and sat down on the bed so that only a few feet separated them. He didn't say anything for a long moment, and when he did his voice was low and somewhat curt. "I don't seem to have much pride where you're concerned. Not enough, anyway, to accept your answer."

She shook her head slightly. "It's impossible. You must see it is so."

"I don't. Trina, I'm sorry for what happened in Germany, and I'm sorry for the way I've acted today. I thought—hell, I didn't think at all. When I saw you again without warning, I knew I still wanted you, that I'd never stopped wanting you. And when you felt something too . . . But that isn't enough, not for us. There's something more between us, even now."

"Wounds."

He hesitated, then nodded jerkily. "I can't deny that. But they were wounds caused by a terrible mistake, and we have to let them heal."

"You wanted revenge," she said, her voice almost inaudible. "You wanted to—to use me."

"No." He made a movement as if he would have reached out to her, but then his hand fell back to clench against his knee. "I know that's how it seemed to you, how it sounded, but I swear I never wanted that. It's just . . . I don't know how you feel, what you're thinking. You're so damned calm, and I—I'm not. But I realized I could still make you want me, and that seemed to be the only way I could reach you."

"What changed your mind?" she asked steadily.

"It hurt too much," he said, his voice rasping over the simple words. Then he cleared his throat and said, "I know I've made you hate me, but please, Trina, give me a chance to change that."

Katrina was struggling, fighting the effect of his voice, his words. She tried not to look at him and yet couldn't tear her eyes from his pale face, seeing in it a glimpse of anguish she wouldn't have believed possible. And that fleeting emotion defeated her in a way his earlier demands could never have.

"I don't hate you."

He reached out quickly and took both her hands in his, holding them tightly. "Then give me another chance."

"You could never forget Germany," she protested, and his reply surprised her.

"I don't want to."

She looked at him mutely, and his grasp on her hands tightened.

"Trina, what happened was my fault. Both of us had secrets, but I'm the one who didn't trust enough to give you at least a chance to explain. I'll regret that for the rest of my life."

She hesitated. "Today you still had doubts about me, and about what I really was in Germany."

"That was six years of bitterness talking." He shook his head, a rueful smile on his lips. "If I'd been able to think at all, I would have known the truth from the moment I first saw you this morning. If you hadn't been one of our agents, or a double agent then, you couldn't be here now. Mueller had you marked a communist agent, which means the CIA would have known the day you entered this country. For you to be living here—and working for Gigi—is cast-iron proof you were never on the other side."

Katrina had no wish to play devil's advocate, but she had to because his belief in the truth was so vitally important. "Unless it was all set up that way," she offered, watching him intently. "The entire point could have been to get me here, and in Gigi's confidence. And that could have been why I married an American."

He was still smiling. "No."

"Why not? It is conceivable."

"Certainly it is," he agreed promptly. "And it's just the sort of devious plan the KGB might have come up with. In fact, they have tried variations of it many times. But Gigi has an infallible instinct, and they've never yet been able to fool her for more than a day or so. Five years? And even before, when she recruited you in Germany? No, you never belonged to the other side."

Very conscious of the warmth and strength of his hands, she tried to draw her own away. "Still—"

He refused to let go. "Trina. We live complicated, suspicious lives, you and I, and it's a rare thing for either of us to trust someone deeply. I know we have to find that kind of trust in each other after what happened in Germany, and I know it won't be easy. But I can't walk away from you without at least *trying*. Not this time."

"Your assignment here—"

"There won't be much happening for the next week or so; you know that. I have to check out the park, all the rides and exhibits, just as a precaution." He hesitated, then added tentatively, "I could use some help, if Gigi can spare you from the hotel."

Katrina gazed at him, and suddenly realized that his eyes were no longer shuttered or hard or reckless; they were more like the eyes she remembered, vivid and filled with life. And she wasn't surprised to hear herself say, "I'll ask."

He lifted one of her hands briefly to his lips and then rose, pulling her to her feet. "I won't push you into anything you're not ready for, Trina."

She half nodded and gently pulled her hands away. "I have to talk to Gigi about the contact I met tonight. So I—I'll see you in the morning."

Skye stood staring at the closed door for a long time before he finally moved. He shrugged off his

jacket and tossed it onto a chair, then loosened his
tie with one hand as he bent and pulled an attaché
case from underneath the bed. The case was locked,
though no combination lock was visible. He sat on
the bed and placed the case on its side, then touched
a sequence of pressure points that were also invisible. The case opened easily.

He studied the contents thoughtfully for a moment, frowning just a little. In cushioned compart-
ments, each separate from the other, reposed a small
bundle of high explosive, a sophisticated timing de-
vice, and an equally sophisticated detonator.

Skye had spent the afternoon exploring the park
casually, and even though his mind had been almost completely fixed on thoughts of Katrina, the
professional part of him had been taking stock unconsciously. And that same professional part of him
now considered and discarded various places he
remembered.

Not the log ride, he thought, or the roller coaster;
both rides allowed far too much random access by
visitors to the park to allow for a specific target—
and the target was very specific. The slower rides
held better possibilities, but they, too, were annoy-
ingly unsuited to his purpose.

How would it be possible, he mused, to target one
person among the thousands in the park at any
given time when the method to be used was explosives? It would be a simple matter, of course, to
blow up an entire area, but Adrian had shown so
much finesse these last few years.

Still frowning, Skye closed the case and returned
it to its place beneath the bed. He had barely straightened again when a soft knock came at the door. He
rose and crossed the room silently, and after a quick

glance through the security spyhole stepped back and opened the door.

"We look odd through that hole," he said.

The gambler, minus his costume, seemed to find nothing strange in the remark. "Do we? I've never noticed." He came into the room and watched Skye shut the door.

"Distorted." Skye looked at him musingly. "Especially you. Must be the mustache. What are you doing on my floor, Dane? If Hagen should see you—"

"Hagen is enjoying his dinner in lonely splendor at the moment. Josh has several of his people on the staff, so we'll be pretty well advised of the great man's movements."

Skye went to the bed and made himself comfortable, leaning back against the headboard. In the same reflective tone he said, "I know the business world would suffer, but Josh really should put his talents to broader use. Between them, he and Raven could straighten out the problems in the United Nations."

Dane grinned a little as he sat on the foot of the bed, but then sobered. "Are you all right?"

Skye looked at his brother's concerned face, identical to his own except for the recent addition of a neat mustache, and smiled a bit wryly. "Yeah. But it's been a hell of a day."

"I got that feeling. The ghost?"

After a slight hesitation Skye said, "I did make a mistake in Germany. She was a double agent, Dane, working for our side."

"What are you going to do about it?" Dane asked quietly.

"Everything I can."

"Guilty conscience?"

"You know better than that." Skye hesitated again,

then added roughly, "Did I ever thank you for keeping me from standing in front of a bullet after Germany?"

Dane looked grave, but his eyes were smiling. "Well, no. As I remember, you tried to knock me down the night I found you. I'm probably being vain in thinking you wouldn't have been able to do it even if you hadn't been pickled at the time."

"Very vain!" Skye retorted, but he was smiling. "It's a bit late, but thanks."

"Don't mention it," Dane responded politely. "I've always wondered, though, what you were doing in Palermo."

Skye was startled. "Was that where you found me?" He had certainly never believed that period of his life was at all amusing, and in fact he and Dane had never talked about it before, but Skye began to realize only then that Dane had very likely had his hands full and deserved much more than a belated thanks.

"You don't remember?"

Beginning to laugh, Skye said, "All I remember is that I woke up on some godawful cargo plane surrounded by crates full of chickens, and that you swore at me until the damned thing landed in Spain. It was Spain, wasn't it?"

Dane half closed his eyes in a wince. "Yes. You gave me the slip half an hour after we landed, and it took me six hours to find you again. It wasn't that hard, all things considered, because all I had to do was ask people if they'd seen me. I got some odd looks, though." He sighed. "You were about to board a tramp steamer headed east, presumably to get back to Palermo. When I tried to grab you, you swung at me and knocked down a dock worker. He wasn't inclined to be amused about the matter, and neither were the officials called in to stop the brawl. We both spent the night in jail, and not much of a jail at that. When I woke up you were gone, having picked the lock and sneaked out while the guard was asleep."

"I do remember that," Skye offered, grinning.

Dane eyed him. "Uh-huh. Do you also remember where I caught up with you a week later?"

"Palermo?"

"Nice try. Casablanca."

It was Skye's turn to wince.

Dane nodded firmly. "Casablanca. I wouldn't have been surprised to find you listening to sad songs, but in fact you were sitting under a tree playing poker with two Bedouins and a very suspicious Turk."

"Did you bring me home then?" Skye asked hopefully.

Dane refused to laugh. "You had just bet everything in your pockets—and lost. The Turk was, to put it mildly, upset to find your pockets empty. By the time I got him placated, *my* pockets were empty, and I had one hell of a time arranging transportation back to the States."

Skye cleared his throat. "I didn't give you any more trouble, did I?"

"None to speak of." He reflected, then decided to speak. "Of course, it would have been a more comfortable trip if you hadn't been hell-bent on getting away from me."

Skye was smiling a little. "Sorry. I wasn't thinking too clearly at the time."

Dane nodded. "I know. I knew then, even though you wouldn't talk about it. Just don't put me through that again, will you?"

"God, I hope not!" He laughed suddenly. "It wasn't amusing at the time, and I'll bet you felt like shooting me. I have to admit it sounds funny now, though. Maybe I'll let you tell Katrina about it one day."

Smiling, Dane got to his feet. "When do Jenny and I meet her?"

"Give me a little time to get to know her again. We're both different after six years. We have a lot of catching up to do, and quite a few things to put behind us."

"Does she know you're a twin?"

Skye nodded. "Since you weren't working with me in Germany, I told her."

"I'd wish you luck," Dane said a bit dryly, "but you already have more of that than any man I know. Now that you have another chance with Katrina, maybe you'll stop wasting your luck by stepping in front of stray bullets and angry bulls."

When his brother had gone, Skye remained where he was for a while, thinking. Dane's final words stuck in his mind, and he realized ruefully that his brother hadn't been deceived six years earlier—or in the time since. It didn't really surprise him.

Ties of blood, ties of love. The bond with his brother would never be broken, and the bond with Katrina had resisted all his wild, bitter, painful attempts to break it.

Now if he could only reach her. . . .

Three

Katrina was up early the next morning. It was her habit to wake before the sun, and the staff of the hotel's smallest restaurant always had coffee and fruit ready for her when she came down from her suite. Today, as usual, she sat in her accustomed booth near the huge windows on the east side of the building, drinking her coffee and watching the sunrise. She had finished her breakfast, and the remains had been taken away.

Two things she no longer took for granted: fresh fruit and sunrises.

"Good morning," Skye said. "May I?"

A bit startled by his sudden appearance, she looked at him and nodded, murmuring a greeting while he slid into the booth across from her. Her restless night and the events of yesterday had left her wary and uncertain, and she didn't quite know how to react to him today.

But Skye, his eyes bright and apparently rested despite the early hour, seemed perfectly friendly. "You used to sleep late," he observed in a light tone.

"Things change," she offered lamely.

He didn't probe. "True. Do I have a companion for the day, or has Gigi chained you to your desk?"

He was giving her an out, she realized, and she knew that if she claimed she had too much work to do, he wouldn't press her. Katrina hesitated, then smiled. "One of the assistant managers will cover for me."

He nodded, obviously pleased. "I'm glad." Then briskly he asked, "Do you have any ideas as to where Adrian might decide to ambush the governor while he's here?"

A bit relieved at the businesslike topic, she considered the matter, returning his gaze thoughtfully as he sipped his coffee and waited. "Anywhere, if he isn't particular about killing innocent people."

"But he is," Skye reminded her. "Or, at least, he has been recently. He's pulled off two hits in the last few months, both against very specific targets. That ambassador in Naples, and the general in Tangier. In both cases only his intended victims were killed."

She shook her head. "But in a crowded theme park? How could he hope to single out one target when he means to use explosives?"

Skye looked reflective. "The governor visits every year, doesn't he?"

"Yes."

"Does he have any favorite rides or exhibits?"

Remembering suddenly, Katrina nodded. "Several. The Haunted Mansion, the pirate ship, the Circus, and the big Ferris wheel. He never misses those."

"Then we concentrate there."

"But the problem is the same. There are always lots of people around. Does it have to be explosives?"

"That was the threat," Skye said. "And Adrian never makes empty threats. It amuses him to watch his intended victims take every possible precaution before he gets them."

She grimaced. "A complete villain."

"He isn't a nice boy," Skye agreed dryly, then immediately went on. "The sun's up, and we have a few hours before the park opens. Want to get started?"

Katrina nodded and slid from the booth, stretching absently in the natural and unconscious movement of one early in the morning. Then she saw Skye looking at her with suddenly darkened eyes as he rose, and she hastily began moving toward the door. "Where to first?" she asked, disturbed at the breathless sound of her own voice.

"The Haunted Mansion is closest," he said steadily.

"Right." Very conscious of him at her shoulder, of his size and the curiously fluid grace of his stride, she walked with him out of the restaurant.

Sometime during the dark predawn hours Katrina had faced the inescapable realization that she felt too much for the man now walking silently beside her. Unwilling to define those feelings, she nevertheless knew there was something primal about them, something far stronger than her memories of what had once existed between them. Before, she had been emotionally young and innocent in many ways, still more girl than woman, and with a girl's recklessness. The passion between them had been astonishingly powerful, the pleasure she found in his arms intense beyond anything she'd ever imagined, yet she knew, looking back, that her very youth and inexperience coupled with the brief time they'd had together had protected her heart.

She had loved, but Skye had been right in believing that how much she had loved could be questioned. Knowing the answer now, she faced it. She had loved him with a girl's unconscious, unaware selfishness, and the loss of him, though agonizing, had not been crippling. She had survived.

But now . . . These feelings frightened her. They were too powerful, too compelling. It was desire she felt, but much more than that, sharper, more primitive, essential. Her mind was in turmoil, wary and confused, yet her body and instincts responded to him on a level deeper than anything she had ever felt.

She was no longer a girl, and she knew without question that her woman's heart could not be touched only lightly. Lessons in survival had built a wall around her heart and soul, and if she loved again, that wall would fall into ruins. If she loved him again—if, in the end, he left her again—there would be no surviving that loss.

"Katrina?"

She looked up at him and felt the breath catch in her throat, vaguely aware that they had reached the Haunted Mansion. In spite of the space separating them as they stood there, she could feel the heat of his big body and the sheer physical power that was like a living force inside him. She slid her hands into the pockets of her jeans, and fought desperately to ignore the fierce pull of compulsive attraction.

"Sorry. My mind was—miles away. How do you want to go about this?" Her voice sounded normal to her.

He shook his head slightly, as if throwing off some thought, and said, "First, the way the governor would—as a park visitor going on a ride."

"I'll start it up," she said, moving away from him.

Skye remained where he was, watching her walk toward a side door of the big Victorian mansion. He had told himself he could handle this, that he could be with her companionably, but he was finding his control was in little better shape than his pride was where she was concerned. For the first time in years he wished he had Dane's control, but their differing personalities and talents made that a hollow wish.

Skye had little of his brother's patience, virtually none of his tranquility, and where Dane was cautious, Skye was all too often reckless to the point of madness.

It did no good at all for Skye to tell himself that it would take care and caution this time to build the necessary trust between him and Katrina. And it was useless to remind himself that if he moved too quickly he could lose her forever. That was what he was afraid of—losing her. And because of that fear all his instincts urged him to grab her and hold on tight. His own nature demanded swift action. It quite simply wasn't in him to play a waiting game for very long; he had too many instincts of the hunter.

Just as his first savage impulse had been to make her respond to him physically, his compulsion now was to see beneath her composure and find the primitive emotions he felt himself. He knew he could reach her through passion. He knew it because he had seen and felt her response to him. And no matter how reasonably his mind warned of the dangers of following that path, he was fighting a losing battle with himself.

He moved finally toward the main door of the mansion, remembering how she had looked in the restaurant as she had stretched lazily. Lord, she was beautiful! Her fiery hair was confined in a single braid hanging down her back; her slender body, clothed in snug jeans and a knit top, was sexier than any other woman's he'd ever seen. It was all he could do to make his voice and words casual when he was with her, and he knew himself too well to believe he could keep himself from touching her for much longer.

She came out of the side door and walked to join him at the main entrance, composed as always. "I've turned on the power," she told him. "The switch is inside beside the first car. Just get in and throw the lever, and the entire system is activated."

"Come with me," he said.

Katrina backed up a step, then drew herself up rather stiffly. "I'd rather not," she said. "This isn't a . . . a favorite ride of mine."

He reached out and took her hand firmly, leading her through the doorway despite her slight resistance. "You can explain the system while we go through it," he said reasonably. "The cars are designed for two anyway," he added as they saw the line of silently waiting vehicles perched on the double track that wound through the house.

"Skye, I'd rather not," she said steadily.

If he had paused a moment to think, he would have realized why she was reluctant, but her hesitation seemed to him to be a desire to avoid being close to him, and his impulsive temper was ignited. "Get in," he ordered roughly.

She glanced up at his face just once, then silently got into the car and sat on the padded seat, her hands clasped together tensely in her lap. He joined her and reached out to throw the switch that set the car in motion.

The half-shell-shaped car jolted forward, banging through a set of swinging doors and plunging into darkness. Skye heard a gasp beside him, and realized then, in a stark instant, what he was doing to her.

Oh, God! She hated enclosed places!

Especially when they were dark.

Swearing at his own insensitivity, he slipped an arm around her in the small car and held her tightly to his side, feeling her stiffen even more as eerie howls and moans erupted from the darkness all around them. The car wasn't moving very fast, but Skye didn't know where the nearest exit was and doubted that Katrina did; it wouldn't diminish her fears at all if they left the car and tried feeling their way blindly to an exit.

So he could only hold her and curse himself.

The car wound jerkily through the huge house, moving from total darkness through a variety of weirdly lighted rooms while various creatures leaped out at them and keening sounds echoed off the walls. In some of the rooms dioramas with mechanical figures acted out bizarre scenes, while in others the projected images of ghostly inhabitants danced or ate serene meals.

Skye thought the ride would never end, and the moment their car bumped against the others waiting patiently in the lighted entrance hall he climbed out, pulling Katrina with him—and straight into his arms.

"I'm sorry," he said thickly, holding her tense, shaking body hard against his own. "God, I'm so sorry."

"It's all right." She tried to push herself back away from him, but he wouldn't release her.

"No, it isn't all right, dammit! Trina, I just didn't stop to think. My bloody temper . . . I wanted you with me, and I—" He had a vivid memory from their days together six years ago of her terror of closets and tiny rooms, particularly dark ones. Now he realized that the months she had spent in prison had very probably made those fears even stronger.

She looked up at him, her amber eyes only beginning to lose the look of terror. "I should have gotten over it by now, but . . . It was the cell in Germany and they turned out the lights so early . . . I've finally gotten used to elevators—" She caught her breath, her mouth firming as she stopped the disjointed words and held the fear at bay. "I'm all right now," she finished in a much steadier voice.

Skye didn't let her go. Hating himself for what he'd put her through, what little control he had managed was now gone. His body was reacting to her closeness wildly, and only the ache in his jaw made him realize that his teeth were tightly clamped together. He forced out words that emerged hoarsely. "I'm a thoughtless bastard, sweetheart, but I never meant to hurt you."

"I know." She sounded uncertain suddenly, gazing up at him with dawning awareness.

The soft pressure of her breasts against his chest inflamed his senses, and he half closed his eyes in a pleasure that was pain. "Lord, you feel so good against me. Trina . . ."

Katrina couldn't move. The urgency of his voice and words sent a flare of heat through her body until it settled deep in her belly to torment her. She felt her lower body move of its own volition, seeking, pressing against him, and a gasp tore from her throat when his body hardened instantly.

Skye made a rough sound and bent his head, his mouth finding hers in a kiss so deep and filled with need it was almost like a blow. Katrina would have collapsed if he hadn't been holding her so tightly, all her senses spinning in a dizzying rush. He was starving, she was starving, and the blood ran through her veins like fire.

She had forgotten this—or had it been like this before? She didn't know, couldn't remember. All she could do was feel. The stark power of his big, hard body made her shockingly frail, and the heat of him burned her. *What a life force he had.* Her body, moving against his hardening loins unconsciously, recognized only the raw virility it craved so helplessly.

But she tried to think, tried to remember the price she could be called upon to pay for this heedless passion, and when his lips left hers finally she managed a whispered protest. "No. No, Skye, it's too soon."

"It was almost too damned late," he said harshly against her throat, his mouth moving caressingly, his tongue touching the pulse hammering beneath her soft flesh. "Six years . . ." His fingers found the elastic band holding the end of her braid and plucked it away, causing her unruly hair to swiftly unwind itself as though it were alive.

Katrina couldn't remember sliding her arms around his waist, but her hands were somehow probing the rippling muscles of his back through his black T-shirt, and when he widened his legs and pressed harder against her she felt her fingers dig into him.

"I want you," he said gutturally, lifting his head. His blazing eyes caught her dazed stare and his arms were like iron around her.

She shook her head, unable to look away. "I can't think. Please, Skye, don't push me! You said you wouldn't—"

His mouth twisted. "I know what I said. I even meant it. But this waiting is killing me."

"Waiting? We met again less than twenty-four hours ago," she protested, and the truth of that made her husky voice honestly indignant.

Skye couldn't help but laugh. "I know, I know."

Another truth—he was bent on sweeping her off her feet a second time—gave Katrina both the strength and the will to push herself away from him. She couldn't help realizing, though, that she escaped his hold only because he chose to let her. "You think it's just a matter of time, don't you?" she demanded.

"We both know it is," he said in a taut voice.

"No, you're wrong." She thought of giving way to him and to her own passion, and the fear of that made her voice shake.

"Am I? I know what you were feeling a moment ago, Trina, because I was feeling it too." His hands clenched into fists at his sides, muscles bulging in his arms.

Katrina felt her breath catch in her throat, and a hot shiver rippled through her body. She hadn't fought the feelings between them six years before, and so she had never seen this side of him. His intensity was a palpable force, reaching out to her, pulling at her. He was impatient, a little rough, almost primitive. He wanted her, and he wasn't prepared to wait much longer.

Wait. He knew they'd be lovers in the end, no matter how much she protested.

She tried to speak evenly. "I'm not denying that, Skye. I can't. But I'm not—not impulsive anymore. I have to be sure this time."

His jaw tightened suddenly. "You weren't last time?"

Katrina hesitated. "I thought I was. I loved you. But I was very young, and we had so little time together. Since then I've learned how important it is to be sure of how I feel."

"You want me," he stated bluntly. "And it's real, Trina."

"Yes." Her voice was soft. "But is passion all? Is it all we're both feeling? If you want only that—"

"What?" His eyes were glittering with a hard light.

"You'll spread your legs willingly, sweet? Throw the dog a bone so he'll stop yapping in your ears?"

She stepped back jerkily.

Immediately Skye said, "Dammit, I didn't mean—" He broke off, flushing.

Katrina was so angry she couldn't speak for a moment, and when she forced the words out, her voice was deceptively mild. "If you want to search this house with all the lights on, the switch is over there on the wall. I'll go check out the big Ferris wheel." She turned and walked out the door.

Dane was up unusually early, and he was already wearing his gambler's costume as he wandered through the park. He knew his restlessness was due partly to Skye; despite his casual attitude the previous night, Dane hadn't been deceived into believing that his brother's troubles were all behind him. The wounds men and women inflict on each other rarely heal quickly, and Skye's own impatience when it came to getting what he wanted was apt to make him act before thinking.

Because those insights were much on his mind as he walked, Dane's first glimpse of the beautiful woman sitting near the Ferris wheel was accompanied by an almost instinctive recognition.

Katrina.

Skye had said little about her since the tragedy of Germany, but Dane remembered his brother's letter announcing his marriage more than six years before. And he had no doubt, as he walked toward her, that this woman with the long, wild red curls and amber cat's eyes was Skye's ex-wife.

She was mad as hell, too, he realized, noting the sparks in those yellow eyes and the firm set of her lips. He wondered what she would make of him, and curiosity as well as the desire to help his brother if he could made up his mind to meet her now.

She looked up as he neared, her eyes widening and then narrowing swiftly, both startled and speculative. And when she spoke, her faintly husky, surprisingly gentle voice was at odds with the lingering temper in her gaze. "You're Dane."

He smiled, stopping before her. "Yes. And you're Katrina."

She looked him up and down with a total lack of self-consciousness. "Identical," she said wryly. "I couldn't believe it when he told me."

"I'm told it's a bit hard to get used to," he offered.

It had taken Katrina almost an hour to check the structure and all the cars of the Ferris wheel, and she was still furious when she had finally sat down on a bench near the ride. Now, looking up at the almost mirror-image of Skye—there was a mustache, but it didn't make Dane look very different—she tried to control her still boiling anger. "He's told you about me, I see."

"Oh, yes," Dane answered mildly. His smile held a softer charm than Skye's, and his voice was lazier.

She studied him curiously, surprised to feel instantly comfortable with him. There was none of the prickling awareness she felt around Skye, and something told her that this brother had a great deal more patience and perhaps more kindness in him. "You and Skye are very different, aren't you?"

"Very," he agreed, still smiling but with a serious gleam in his eye. Then, sympathetically, he added, "My brother can be a difficult man at times. I don't mean to be nosy, but since you're obviously mad as hell, I gather you two have had a fight?"

It wasn't in Katrina's nature to confide easily, but she was so angry that didn't seem to matter. Remembering Skye's crude words, she winced. "You could say that."

"He has a touchy temper," Dane said in a judicious tone, "and he doesn't always stop to think before he speaks." Then, quietly, he said, "Especially when his heart is involved."

Katrina looked away from those forceful eyes. It was another difference between the brothers, she realized. In Dane, that amazingly strong life force was confined in his eyes, but in Skye it was diffused throughout his entire powerful body. She tried a laugh that didn't quite come off. "He obviously hasn't told you everything if you believe his heart's involved."

"He didn't have to tell me," Dane said simply.

Torn between the need for reassurance and her wariness of the strong emotions Skye could awaken in her, she looked back at Dane's grave face uncertainly.

After a moment Dane said, "Skye's spent a lot of time in the dark these last years—in more ways than one. He hasn't let himself feel very much since Germany, but I believe seeing you again has made splinters of the protective wall he'd built around his emotions. It must feel like being caught in a sudden storm without warning. So if he seems impatient or even rough, maybe you should remember that you can hurt him every bit as much as he can hurt you."

Katrina shook her head slightly and fixed her gaze on the ground, unwilling to believe that.

Dane sighed, and his voice was rueful. "I can see you're as stubborn as he is. I shouldn't be surprised, I suppose. It'll take a hardheaded woman to manage my brother."

Her hard head came up hastily, and she stared at him.

"He needs it, you see," Dane told her solemnly.

"It's been my job off and on for the better part of thirty-five years, but I have a wife now, and she's keeping me too busy to give me much time to cope with Skye's recklessness." A bit more seriously he added, "He needs a balance, a center. He needs someone to care about him, so he'll stop and think before risking his neck."

She refused to be moved by the words, ignoring a sudden pang near her heart. "I don't think he needs anything or anyone," she said flatly. "He's too strong to need."

One of Dane's eyebrows lifted and his eyes hardened. "Is he? Even strong men can be shattered if the blow's hard enough and the aim is good. He isn't made of iron, Katrina."

She felt absurdly in the wrong. "I know."

"Good. Convince him, will you?" Dane smiled suddenly, the flinty look gone from his eyes. Before she could respond, he added a light "See you," and moved gracefully away.

Katrina stared after him for a few moments, then fixed her eyes on the pavement again and tried to get her thoughts and emotions under control. She found it hard to accept that Skye felt something other than desire for her, though she had felt that desire and knew only too well how powerful it was.

Vaguely aware of faint sounds and movements as the park was readied for the day's visitors, she struggled to come to terms with her own feelings. Could she accept the passion between her and Skye without looking farther? No. She knew herself too well. It wasn't in her to give her body without giving her heart as well, and she was afraid of the very idea of giving her heart to Skye.

And she didn't know what he wanted. Another

chance? What did that mean? *Because I've never been able to forget you. Even when I wanted to.*

She was beginning to realize, partly due to Dane, that she had never really known Skye. She hadn't looked deeply enough six years earlier. He wasn't a tender man, or even a gentle man; he was too forceful to be either for very long, and she no doubt would have discovered that years before if they'd had more time together. He was hard in many ways, and he could be cruel. His life had taught him to be suspicious, and probably to expect the worst. His temper was as quick as the remorse he felt afterward, both expressed hastily and in blunt words.

But she hadn't seen that six years earlier.

Startling herself by speaking wryly aloud, Katrina murmured, "You fell in love with a beautiful face." She shook her head, no longer surprised that Skye had gotten her totally off balance this time, because now she was looking underneath that beautiful face, and the unexpected force of him was shocking in its intensity.

How could she have been so blind all those years before? So shallow that she had never even tried to understand him? Even though they'd had little time, she should have *seen*.

And now . . . Now she was older, and wiser, and always strove to see beneath the surface. She was a woman, and the instincts that had never stirred at twenty-two were torturing her.

He was complex and often rough, and his impulsive temper had already cut her more than once. But the strength and force in him tugged at her like nothing she'd ever felt before, and the sheer primitive passion he aroused in her left her weak and shaking in his arms.

She didn't hear him then, but looked up anyway

as Skye approached her rapidly. His expression was stony, and there was so much leashed violence in his pantherlike stride that for a moment she felt a thrill of fear. But then he yanked her up from the bench and into his arms, and his muttered words chased the fear away.

"I'm sorry. I didn't mean it, Trina, I swear I didn't." His head was bowed, and he rubbed his cheek against her hair. "God, I keep saying that to you, don't I?"

She lifted her face from his shoulder and smiled, wondering dimly what had happened to her anger. "It's probably good for you," she said.

His eyes moved restlessly over her face and his mouth twisted in self-contempt. "I don't know what I'm saying half the time around you. You make me feel like some horny teenager with sweaty hands. I keep hurting you."

"I'll keep your temper in mind from now on," she said a bit ruefully. "But what you said didn't hurt me, it made me mad." Her chin came up. "You had no right to say that."

"I know." He hesitated, then asked, "Will you tell me something honestly, Trina?"

She felt wary, but nodded.

"Has there been anyone since me?"

Katrina couldn't look away, and she couldn't lie to him. Not about this. "No."

"Once burned?" he suggested in an obviously false light voice.

She wasn't ready to be that honest. "I've been very busy," she said evasively, stepping back and feeling both relief and disappointment when he instantly released her.

His eyes gleamed. "So I shouldn't imagine you've been eating your heart out for me all these years, huh?"

"I wouldn't if I were you," she returned dryly, grateful that he was treating this casually. Then he shook her up again by refusing to let the matter drop.

"Still," he said, watching her intently. "Six years is a long time for a beautiful woman to be alone."

"Five," she snapped. "You forgot prison."

His faint smile died. "I keep trying to forget it, but I can't. Did they hurt you, Trina?"

"Not a mark," she said flippantly, back on balance. He caught her hand when she would have turned away. "I have to know," he said in a harsh voice.

She looked at him for a moment, then said, "Interrogation techniques are more subtle these days, you know that. Drugs, sensory deprivation. And there wasn't much I *could* tell them, after all. They didn't really suspect me of being a double agent, they just wanted to know about you. I came through it."

"You should hate me," he said slowly.

"Because of them? I knew the risks. I never blamed you for that, Skye, because it wasn't your fault." She held her voice steady with an effort. "Is that why you want another chance? Because you feel guilty?"

"No. No, that isn't why."

"Then there's nothing more to say about it. Did you find anything in the Haunted Mansion?"

"Back to business?"

"I think we'd better." She could hear the strain in her voice and wasn't surprised by it. She felt buffeted by the storm of emotions that had swept over her during the last twenty-four hours, and didn't know how much more she could take.

Skye must have heard the strain as well, because his expression softened abruptly and he carried her hand to his lips before releasing it. "All right," he said gently. "I'll try to stop pushing."

She nodded, wishing she didn't feel like crying

when he showed her a rare glimpse of his softer side. "Did you find anything?" she repeated.

"No. How about you?"

"Nothing. The park will open in an hour; we don't have time to go over the pirate ship or the circus tent today."

"There's no hurry. But since you've got the day off, why don't you show me around the park?"

"You've seen it," she objected somewhat weakly.

"Not with you." He smiled. "I promise to be good."

Katrina wasn't sure she trusted his smile, but she wanted to be with him and couldn't deny it even to herself.

For the next three days Skye kept his promise, and Katrina's wariness soon eased. He didn't bring up the past or push her in any way, and since he was an extremely charming man when he put his mind to it, she was quickly disarmed—and was aware of the ease with which he'd accomplished it.

She had refused to abandon her duties for more than one day, though, and Skye hadn't protested. Instead, he turned up often during the day, joining her for meals and spending a few minutes talking to her in her office. Some of the talk was of business, but for the most part the conversations were casual and friendly. He took her to dinner each night, danced with her, and left her at her door with a light kiss.

"Biding his time, isn't he?" Gigi, amused, asked as she passed Katrina in the lobby one morning just after Skye had been talking to her.

Katrina had to smile, because Skye's determined patience was so obvious it was almost funny. But she felt no impulse to laugh; she was grateful to him for giving her time, especially when she could sense the strain lurking just under his composure.

And that it was a strain on him she didn't doubt; it was in his voice sometimes, and in his face there was a finely honed look. He was an impatient man by nature, so the fact that he was forcing himself to be undemanding said a great deal about his determination to develop a new relationship with her.

She appreciated that deeply, but it was a strain on her, too, because she was no closer to sorting out her own feelings, and the pull of physical attraction was growing stronger with every passing day. She was afraid that desire was clouding her judgment, and she didn't know how to cope with it.

She could feel his presence the instant he entered a room, even if her back was to him, and when he was with her she found it almost impossible to look at anything but him.

On the third day it occurred to her with devastating simplicity that she was falling in love with him.

She was sitting at her desk, conscious of the faint smile that Skye had left her with just minutes before, and when the realization dropped into her mind it did so with the clarity of total certainty.

I'm beginning to love him.

She put her pen down with unnatural care and folded her hands on her neat desk blotter, conscious of her heart beating like a drum in her ears. She felt both hot and cold, eager and fearful, delighted and hurting. She hadn't meant to love him. He had crept into her heart with charm and patience.

And she couldn't let him know, because she was still afraid of giving him her heart.

Despite his careful patience these last days, Katrina knew only too well that the power of his desire for her was an all-consuming thing, stark and possessive. Whatever his feelings for her now, he wouldn't be content with only a "loving and passionate" woman in his bed. He would demand a total surrender this time, driven by his own doubts about the depths of her feelings before to be certain of them now.

Beginning to understand him, Katrina knew that his harsh demands on that first night had not been uttered only with the desire to exact revenge for what he had gone through after Germany. There had been a certain amount of truth in his avowed intention to purge himself of her.

She wondered if he realized himself what he was after this time.

He had gone through hell after Germany; she didn't doubt that. In all truth, he had been more deeply hurt than she had, because the shallowness of her own emotions had protected her somewhat, and because she had known there had been no betrayal. For six years Skye had remembered her, his own feelings eating at him. Then they had met again, against all odds, and he was bent on a "second chance."

Katrina couldn't help but believe that whether or not Skye knew it himself, what he wanted was to get her out of his system once and for all. So she couldn't very well tell him she loved him.

She *couldn't.*

Four

Teddy Steele began to push herself into a sitting position on the bed, but then turned somewhat green and hastily fell back onto the pillows. The very powerful arm of her husband reached out with perfect timing, and a cracker was placed between her lips. Teddy didn't waste time with thanks, but munched the cracker with her eyes closed, willing her stomach to settle.

Zach raised himself on an elbow and looked down at his wife's pale face with a worried frown. "Better, honey?"

One of her big brown eyes opened cautiously, then the other, and she sighed in relief as her stomach behaved. Blinking away the morning dryness of her contact lenses, she answered, "Yes, but it's the pits."

"Why don't you sleep in today?" he suggested casually.

Teddy eyed him with loving understanding, her gamine's smile quirking her lips. "I'm fine, Zach." She reached up a hand to his lean cheek, stroking gently. "I'm not going to lose this one."

Zach had a great deal of faith in his vivacious wife's peculiar psychic certainties, but he had too much experience with the vagaries of fate to share her confidence. He also remembered far too vividly Teddy's miscarriage months before, and the terror he'd gone through at almost losing her. Not all her assurances—or those of the doctor who was still astonished by this second conception—could allay his fears. He caught her hand and held it firmly to his face, his free hand moving to push the sheet aside and cover her very slightly rounded belly. "You should have stayed in New York," he said a bit harshly.

"What, and miss our final hurrah?" she said, deliberately light. "It isn't a jungle this time, remember? There's no danger at all, Zach."

He shook his head slightly. "Honey, there's always danger in a scheme like ours. We've covered all the bases, sure, but it's impossible to plan for the unexpected element. And Hagen's such a wild card, God only knows what could happen."

"Well, you're with me," she said serenely, her faith in her big warrior absolute.

His lips twisted, but his gray eyes gleamed with sudden wry humor, and she grinned at him. Zach bent his head to kiss her, his hand still moving gently over her stomach. After a few moments he muttered huskily, "We should have waited, given you more time to recover."

Teddy, perfectly aware that his mind was never long distracted from her unexpected pregnancy, slid her arms around his neck and laughed softly. "After you and the other guys came back into the country on that flying visit, I was so happy to see you that birth control never crossed my mind. Or yours, for that matter."

Remembering the very passionate reunion with his wife, Zach silently admitted that his lifelong control had never stood against Teddy. Thank heaven. Aloud, he said, "Are we going to tell her she was conceived in a Jeep?"

Solemnly Teddy said, "Well, if I'd known neither of us could wait until we got home, I would have borrowed the limo to pick you up at the airport. Then she could have been conceived in style."

He chuckled softly. "And I probably wouldn't have given a damn about the driver either." He caught his breath suddenly as her hand wandered, and added somewhat thickly, "Didn't the doctor say we should be careful?"

"I plan to be extremely careful," Teddy said. "We have a couple of hours before we meet the others in Josh and Raven's suite for breakfast. That's long enough to be careful, don't you think?"

Zach, no longer unnerved by his inability to think at all where his wife was concerned, growled and pulled her petite body into his arms.

Skye walked briskly along the paved pathway leading to the Old West section of the park. The gates hadn't opened for the day, but he could hear the usual morning noises, and employees in costumes wandered about talking and laughing. From the section Skye was nearing came occasional gunfire as various characters practiced the tricks they'd be called upon to perform later.

Stopping to watch two costumed characters perfecting their sharpshooting, Skye waited for a pause in the gunfire and then said dryly, "Funny how many of you have managed to act out your own personal fantasies."

Lucas Kendrick, in the guise of Wild Bill Hickok, chuckled as he reloaded his rifle. "My ego's suffering," he told the other man, and nodded at the slim brunette at his side who wore the costume of Annie Oakley. "She's so much better than I am."

Kyle's turquoise eyes gleamed briefly at her husband, and then she looked at Skye. "Something up?"

He shook his head. "Not really. But I've settled on the Ferris wheel as the most likely spot."

Lucas turned to look in the direction of the Ferris wheel, his sharp blue eyes narrowing as he picked out the tall structure in the distance. "Good," he murmured thoughtfully. "It's fairly central, so we can all get there quickly."

"Will you tell the others?" Kyle asked Skye.

"Yeah." Skye listened intently as the sounds of gunfire echoed, and added, "If you two see Raven and Josh, tell them, will you? They're the only ones who wander all over the park, and I may not see them anytime soon."

"Sure." Lucas gazed at him steadily. "You sound a bit jumpy."

Skye managed a shrug. "Must be the gunfire. See you later." He strode off.

Lucas looked at his wife with a lifted brow, and she said, "I caught it too. He's definitely on edge."

Grimacing slightly, Lucas said, "I've noticed Dane's keeping a pretty close eye on him, and he wouldn't if he weren't worried about his brother. If Hagen sees those two together, he's going to start to smell a rat."

"They're both pros," she observed.

He nodded, but said, "Still, one thread too tight and this whole thing's going to unravel. Maybe we'd better talk to the others tonight."

Kyle nodded agreeably, then took aim with her

rifle and put yet another neat hole through the target some yards away. Lucas gave her a pained look, but laughed warmly.

Meanwhile, Skye found the others he sought gathered around the sheriff's office in the dusty main street of the Old West town. The sheriff, a tall, lean man with copper hair and tawny eyes and a lazy air that was somewhat deceptive, straightened from his lounging pose to offer Skye a cheerful hello.

Skye returned the greeting as he looked at him, then eyed the other three people. Both the ladies were tiny, and both were redheads, but the sheriff's lady had an expression of serenity in her sea-green eyes that perfectly matched both her husband's lazy calm and her own dignified costume of schoolteacher. The other redheaded lady, leaning back against the gunslinger who had both arms around her, had big, waiflike brown eyes that were bright with interest and a vivid face that made her as eye-catching as the scanty saloon girl costume she wore.

Looking finally at the powerful dark man who was playing the role of gunslinger, a menacing figure due to his size, the faint scar on his lean cheek, and the all-black costume, Skye shook his head ruefully. "You people didn't choose this park just because of Adrian's threat," he said definitely. "You wanted the chance to play dress-up."

Teddy Steele giggled engagingly. "No, because the guys would have worn commando outfits. It took me all of an hour to talk Zach into being the villain."

A deep chuckle rumbled from the gunslinger, and his powerful arms tightened gently around his wife. "This isn't so bad," he commented to Skye in an unexpectedly soft voice. "But I feel for Josh."

Rafferty Lewis laughed as well, pushing his white hat to the back of his head. "Face it, we're all having fun with this. Even Josh. Better than a vacation. What's up, Skye?"

Skye repeated his decision to settle on the Ferris wheel as the site of the governor's attempted assassination, leaning back against a hitching post as he spoke to them. Their reaction was much the same as Lucas's and Kyle's.

"When does the balloon go up?" Teddy asked.

"A week from Saturday, if all goes well," Skye answered. "Right on schedule." He felt an unusually steady gaze on him, and looked at the schoolteacher, whose eyes were gentle.

"Are you all right?" she asked.

He managed a smile. "Fine, Sarah." He knew his control was strained to the breaking point, but until he had talked to Lucas and Kyle he'd believed he was hiding it well. Obviously not. Before anybody else could mention it, he said, "I'll try to touch base with the others sometime today. Hagen said something about seeing the Wild West show, but I'll try to keep him busy. Better stay alert, though."

"Thanks for the warning," Zach said.

Skye saluted them casually and left.

There was a moment of silence after he'd gone, and then Teddy said reflectively, "Does anybody know if we're unintentionally matchmaking?"

Sarah looked at her. "It was that kind of tension, wasn't it?"

"I'd say so. And, according to Raven, Skye isn't the type to get nervous professionally. This operation has to be a piece of cake to him. So what other reason could there be?"

Rafferty sighed. "If we've learned anything by now, it has to be that where Hagen is, romance is. Against all odds. It isn't really any of our business, though," he added carefully.

"No." Zach's deep voice was slow and thoughtful. "But if that's the cause of Skye's tension, he isn't handling it well. And he's the linchpin of the entire plan. Dane could step in, I suppose, if it comes to that. Maybe we'd better find out what's going on."

Rafferty eyed his large friend. "Well, you ask Skye, then. You're about the only one of us big enough to take him on if he doesn't like the question."

"Raven," Sarah said in her soft, serene voice. "She knows him better than we do. Leave it to her."

Teddy nodded quick agreement. "We can talk to her about it tonight."

Zach looked at Rafferty and nodded as well. "It might be best. And she may know what's going on already."

They all heard the loud whistle announcing the imminent opening of the park's gates, and Zach added wistfully to the sheriff, "Can't I shoot you today?"

Rafferty pulled his white hat firmly back down and adjusted the gun on his hip. "Don't be ridiculous. I'm the good guy."

"Shyster," Zach said rudely, and took his giggling wife's hand to lead her toward the saloon.

Skye decided to keep Hagen busy for the day by getting Gigi's help, and she listened to his suggestion with lifted brows and a tiny smile.

"And why should I?" she asked.

Grinning suddenly, Skye said, "Because he's wandering around the hotel like a beaten hound, that's why. I never thought I could feel sorry for Hagen, but I do. You're a cruel woman, Gigi."

She chuckled. "He needed a lesson. However, that's quite beside the point. Just what are *you* going to be doing while I keep Hagen's mind off visiting the park?"

Skye cleared his throat. "Double-checking a few things." And when she continued to gaze at him with perceptive eyes, he forced himself to sit still in her visitor's chair.

Gently she said, "Today is her usual day off. Did she tell you?"

"No," Skye said a bit grimly.

Ignoring the tone, Gigi explained. "She wanted to work since she took the other day off, but I thought not. Not quite her usual calm self, my Trina; I ordered her to rest."

Skye rose from his chair abruptly but then paused, looking across the desk at the older woman. "Tell me something," he said a bit jerkily. "Am I bad for her?"

"What would you do if I said yes?"

"I don't know."

After a moment Gigi said seriously, "I can't answer your question, Skye. Only Trina can."

He didn't intend to ask Katrina about that, but when she opened her door to him ten minutes later, it was the question uppermost in his mind. She had been less wary these last days, but it seemed to him that whenever he tried to step closer she moved elusively away from him. And both his determined patience and his control over his own desires were wearing thin.

He greeted her abruptly. "We have to talk."

Caution crept into her amber eyes, but she stepped back to allow him to come in. She was in her usual off-duty clothing, jeans and a casual shirt, barefooted and with her glorious hair flowing loosely down her back. He was reminded again of the paradox of her, her innate composure warring with the outward suggestion of wildness.

It has to be there! he thought with more than a hint of the savagery she always inspired in him. It had driven him half mad years before, that conviction of his that locked somewhere inside Katrina was an intensity to match his own, a fiery spirit crying out to be freed. And he had tried to touch that part of her. But although she had responded to him with loving passion, he had been unable to find the vital woman he sensed beneath the calm, smiling eyes.

He was no closer now, and it was still driving him mad. The desire between them was sharper than ever before, but he was all too aware that Katrina was holding herself aloof from him. He looked at the wariness in her eyes as they moved into her den, and he wanted to demand, *Where do you go when you hide from me? Why can't I find you?*

"Is something wrong?" she asked.

He forced a laugh. "Well, since I've had several people who barely know me point out that I'm jittery as hell, I suppose I can't deny it."

"I'm sorry," she said uncertainly. Her arms moved in what seemed a conditioned response, folding over her breasts.

Skye ignored the body language, refusing to be warned off. He took two quick steps to stand before her, pulling her abruptly into his arms. "I can't take much more of this," he said in a voice that grated. "I've tried, Trina, I swear I have."

Her arms had moved by instinct around his waist, and Katrina gasped when the heat of his body pressed against hers. "You—you said we had to talk," she managed to say unsteadily.

"I lied." His eyes were fixed on hers in a hard,

searching stare, and a muscle tightened in his jaw. "We've talked, and it hasn't helped. I've taken cold showers, and it hasn't helped. For the second time I've forgotten I'm a professional, and it's because of you. Again."

"Skye—"

He shifted one hand to her face, holding her as if to keep her still even though she hadn't moved. "Why can't I find it?" he muttered almost to himself.

"What?" She was bewildered.

Without answering, he bent his head and fitted his mouth to hers in a very deliberate movement. His hand slid around to the back of her head, long fingers tangling in her hair as he took her mouth with utter confidence.

Katrina recognized that male certainty in him, but she couldn't deny it because he had every reason to be sure of her response. She was coming apart inside, melting in the stark heat of her need and his, and in the newfound awareness of her own love an overwhelming desire for him jolted through her like pure flame. Her fingers dug into the hard muscles of his back, her body arched into his in a driven need to be closer, and a sound like a primitive wail of desperation knotted in the back of her throat.

It had never been like this before, and she surrendered to it, and him, because there was no choice left to her. With an eagerness she couldn't fight or hide, her mouth came wildly alive beneath his, her arms tightened around him, and the soft contours of her body molded themselves to his hard length.

Skye lifted his head abruptly, his eyes blazing in a way she'd never seen before. "I knew it," he said thickly, satisfaction and an emotion she couldn't name ringing in his voice.

Katrina was too dazed to say anything at all, and she could only gasp when he lifted her easily into his arms and carried her into her bedroom. She was burning, out of control, and at that moment she no longer cared why he wanted her or how long he would want her; he wanted her now, and that was enough.

He lowered her to her feet beside the bed, his hands going instantly to the hem of her shirt and pulling it quickly up and over her head. The shirt was tossed carelessly aside, and Katrina felt her bra fall away before his warm, hard hands surrounded her naked breasts. Her fingers clutched at his muscled arms, and she swayed toward him, a soft moan breaking from her lips as her body responded violently to his touch.

Skye made a rough sound and kissed her, his mouth hot with demand as his hands slid down to cope feverishly with the snap of her jeans. The heavy denim was pushed down over her hips, followed quickly by her wispy panties, and Katrina automatically stepped free of the material that pooled around her feet.

As driven as he was, she tugged at his T-shirt, helping him to peel it off over his head, and she barely had his jeans unfastened when he shoved them down and kicked them violently aside. It was Katrina who stepped back and fell onto the bed, pulling him with her and unconcerned that his weight could have hurt her. But Skye caught most of his weight on his elbows, still kissing her violently. There was no time for gentleness, and no desire for it in either of them. And there was no need for preliminaries, because Katrina was ready for him, desperate for him, and she couldn't wait. She wanted him now, right now, the imperative craving for his possession overpowering and tormenting. She returned his kisses with the same searing hunger he displayed, and her legs were already apart, wrapping around him, her body writhing beneath him.

She cried out wildly as he entered her with a powerful thrust, the sensation briefly unfamiliar and shocking. It had been a long time for her, and he was a big man in every way, but her body adjusted quickly in its own heated need, and she moaned as she felt him throbbing inside her. Through the mists of her urgency she saw his face, taut and almost savage, and then the fire in her was burning out of control and she was moving with him, matching his raw force, hardly aware of the sounds tearing from her throat.

It was quick and hard and primitive, and when release came it left them shuddering and so utterly drained that neither of them could move for a long time. When he did move, Skye simply rolled so that she lay on top of him, and like that, their bodies cooling and still entangled, they both slept deeply.

Katrina woke slowly but she made no effort to move. She listened to his heart beat steadily, aware of his powerful arms wrapped firmly around her and of the slow rise and fall of his chest beneath her cheek. His big, hard body was a surprisingly comfortable bed, and she never wanted to move.

But her mind refused to float lazily for long, and when she remembered her own passion, shock mingled with astonishment. Had that been she? That wild woman so desperate with need she had practically ripped his clothes off? He hadn't even had to demand the total surrender because she'd offered it mindlessly.

And what now? She felt a chill of fear, wondering if he would leave her. Wondering if that fiery, primitive joining had purged him of her once and for all. She bit her lip and unconsciously rubbed her cheek against the soft pelt of black hair beneath it, aching inside.

But she wouldn't let him see that ache. She was a proud woman, a survivor, and she would deal with the anguish of losing him as she had always dealt with pain and loss. Alone. Already, she was calling on the strength that had seen her through the last six years, holding tightly to every shred of dignity.

Skye moved then, and she found herself on her back gazing up at him as he leaned on an elbow above her. The faint smile curving his lips made her heart catch because it held such utter satisfaction, and her eyes skittered away from his, both shy and guarded. Would he say it now?

"Look at me," he ordered softly.

She did, watching his smile die and that hard, searching glitter return to his eyes. It bewildered her.

"Don't hide from me." His voice was suddenly guttural, and a frown drew his brows together. "I won't let you. Not now."

"I don't know what you mean," she whispered.

He stared at her for a moment, then bent his head and kissed her so deeply she was shaking when it finally ended. "That's better," he said, his lips moving over her throat.

Katrina didn't know what he was talking about, but those searching lips were trailing fire wherever they touched, and the embers inside her were beginning to glow with renewed heat. It couldn't be important anyway, she thought, her fingers compulsively probing his shoulders and back. As long as he wasn't going to leave her right away, nothing else was important.

His lips were moving over her breastbone now, and his big hand slid up over her quivering stomach and slowly closed around one swelling mound. She gasped, blinking at the sudden wave of dizziness and heat, forgetting everything but the sensations he was arousing in her body.

Skye's head lifted briefly, his eyes stabbing into hers, and he muttered thickly, "Much better," before lowering his lips to her breast again. She wasn't hiding from him now, her amber eyes flickering with smoldering intensity, her lovely face awakening, growing absorbed in passion, and he was determined to make certain she couldn't slip elusively away from him again.

That retreat had cut him like a knife, especially after the wild lovemaking they'd shared, and he had been conscious of the fierce desire to drive her crazy with wanting him, just as he was crazy with wanting her. Only the sharpest edge of his need had been blunted, and he meant to love her slowly this time and get reacquainted with her body.

Lord, she was beautiful! She had all the slenderness of a model, yet her slim body was curved in all the right places. Her breasts fit his hands perfectly, the coral nipples so sensitive to his touch that a moan jerked from her lips when he tugged at them gently. He watched those responsive buds tighten into hard points as he stroked them with his thumbs, and his own body tautened and pulsed heavily as he aroused her.

"Skye," she murmured throatily, arching up to fit her breasts more firmly into his caressing hands.

"Tell me you want me," he ordered in a rasping voice, bending his head to tease a stiffened nipple with his lips.

Her nails dug into his shoulders and her eyes were alight now, like a cat's in the dark, fierce and untamed. "I want you," she whispered raggedly.

He continued to tease, his tongue flicking her sensitive flesh, his fingers kneading in a slow, lazy motion. But a strangled, impassioned sound from her snapped a thread of his control, and his mouth closed hotly over her nipple. He could feel her shaking, and her deep moan of pleasure made his heart hammer violently against his ribs. One of his hands slid down over her writhing body, and the softness of the red curls he found at the base of her belly yanked a groan from deep in his chest.

"Now?" he demanded urgently, raising his head so he could gaze into her wild eyes. He could feel her readiness, his fingers probing her slick heat, and the power of his own need was snapping the remaining threads of his control.

She tugged at his shoulders mutely, almost sobbing when he spread her legs and moved between them. He gritted his teeth, fighting every instinct urging him to bury himself in her because the sheer pleasure of slowly entering her body was driving him to the edge of madness. And when he settled finally against her, deeply inside her, she held him in a hot, velvety clasp that sent shudders of ecstasy rippling through him.

Her lips curved in a slow, mysterious female smile that held nothing of reserve or composure, and her arms tightened around him in unconscious possession, her hips lifting instinctively to take all of him. He tangled his fingers in her fiery hair and kissed her again and again, catching the soft whimpers

that escaped her as he began moving, at first slowly
and then with gathering speed and force.

Skye was out of control again, and some dim part
of him recognized that he always would be with her,
that his need for her was too primal to allow con-
straints. It burned inside him, seared all his senses,
frantic and savage, and the hoarse sounds that tore
their way out of his tight throat were almost sobs.
He pulled her legs higher around him and drove
deeper into her welcoming heat, blind to everything
but his own critical necessity and the woman who
matched his demand with an equal, passionate need
of her own.

Then she stiffened with an incoherent cry, and
the strong inner contractions of her pleasure caught
him in a mind-numbing caress. He groaned raggedly, his senses exploding with a violence that was
like dying, and lost himself in her.

When he could breathe again, Skye raised himself
slowly on his elbows, concerned that he was too
heavy for her. But she wouldn't let him leave her,
her slender legs tightening around him and a mumbled protest escaping her. He framed her face in his
hands, his thumbs smoothing the flushed, satiny
skin, and he could feel her fingers moving lazily in
his hair. Her eyes opened slowly, darkened now, and
he searched them with an eagerness that was almost painful.

She's still with me. She isn't hiding.

He kissed the swollen curve of her lips, then the
tip of her nose where the three freckles beckoned.
"It's a good thing you have the day off," he said.

She blinked, and the ebbing flush of passion welled
back up in her cheeks for another reason. In an

uncertain voice she said, "We can't stay here all day."

"Why not?" He pushed a lock of fiery hair back off her damp forehead, smiling just a little. But his eyes were watchful.

Katrina was too conscious of the starkly intimate weight of his hard, heavy body covering her own to be able to resurrect her wariness, and after what they had shared on her bed she was too honest to pretend shyness. Her love would remain unspoken, but if this powerful, relentless passion could keep him with her a while longer, she was bound by that love to cherish every moment.

She lifted her head from the pillow and kissed him, her tongue dancing, teasing, and when he caught his breath and his arms wrapped around her, she felt a stab of pleasure in the knowledge that she could excite him so instantly. "Why not?" she agreed huskily against his mouth.

He laughed, a rough sound, and his teeth nipped her bottom lip gently. "All day—and all night. In fact, sweetheart, it'd take a determined army to keep me out of your bed now."

Katrina erected only one barrier in her mind, hiding behind that only her love and inevitable painful thoughts about a future without him. Smiling up at his intent face, she said, "I don't think I could move anyway." And she protested wordlessly when he moved instead to slowly withdraw from her.

Her disappointment was brief, however, because he immediately gathered her into his arms and carried her into the bright, spacious bathroom. He had never carried her six years before, and she was both surprised and moved by the curious emotions his easy strength awoke in her; she felt small and fragile, and oddly cared for even though he wasn't especially gentle with her.

And she wasn't, this time, surprised by the inexorable building of heat that had little to do with the hot water streaming over them as they stood in the glassed-in shower stall. She did find a moment to marvel at his apparently limitless energy, but the soapy hands moving slowly over her wet body very soon stole her ability to think at all.

Standing so close to him, nakedly vulnerable, she was again conscious of his immense physical strength. He could break her so easily, she realized vaguely, her trembling fingers compulsively stroking over the thick, wet pelt of black hair on his chest, his ribs, and hard, flat stomach. He had a natural, almost primal force that few men could boast of, the kind that would require a conscious and iron will to temper.

And though he wasn't gentle with her, he nonetheless reined that vital strength. He handled her body with hunger, yet despite that starkly savage need he had not once hurt her.

He had washed her hair, soaping and rinsing, his long fingers so pleasurable she almost purred aloud. Then, luminous eyes intent, utterly silent, he began stroking her body slowly. Leaning back against him, her eyes closed, Katrina felt the slippery caress of his hands as they lingeringly soaped her swelling, aching breasts, and hot shivers coursed through her.

Her hands went back by reflex to brace herself, and her fingers closed over the hard muscles of his thighs, clenching when his caresses moved down over her ribs and stomach. The pulsing ache between her legs was a sweet torment, and when his palm covered her she almost collapsed, moaning.

Skye muttered something, low and rough, and abruptly turned her around to face him. He pulled her hard against him, his hands sliding down her back to her buttocks, lifting her. Katrina felt the cool tile wall against her back, and her body responded instantly, as always, to his potent urgency. Her legs parted for him jerkily, and her strangled cry lost itself in his mouth as he thrust violently into her.

She clung to him, half sobbing at the almost punishing force her body accepted and craved more of. And even as the hot friction of their passion pushed them rapidly to the brink and over, she faced the stark truth that what she felt for him was more than love, far more basic than desire. He was her match, her mate, she belonged to him body and spirit, and her woman's body had known that with the instant, soul-deep shock of recognition.

He could destroy her.

Almost two hours later Katrina slipped from the wildly mussed bed and found a terry robe in her closet, being as quiet as possible so she wouldn't wake Skye. He was sleeping deeply, his lean face relaxed and vulnerable, and she paused to look at him for a long moment before leaving the bedroom and easing the door closed behind her.

A glance at the wall clock in her kitchenette told her it was mid-afternoon, and a pang from her stomach told her she was hungry. Her cupboard, however, was somewhat bare since it was easier for her to eat most of her meals in the hotel's restaurants. She returned to the den and called room service, ordering coffee and food. Plenty of it.

Skye was still asleep when the order arrived, but

he came out of the bedroom a few minutes later, wearing only his jeans, to find Katrina curled up on a corner of the couch sipping coffee.

He leaned over the back of the couch and tipped her face up with one hand, kissing her. "Hello," he said. "You taste of coffee, sweetheart."

She lifted her cup in a small salute, smiling. "I ordered some food. We missed lunch."

"That," he said, "is a matter of opinion. But I am hungry. Have you eaten yet?"

"No. I waited for you." She watched him move over to the cart holding covered dishes, and a pang sharper than any she'd ever known made her catch her breath in silent anguish.

What was it Dane had said? That his brother needed someone to care for him so that he'd stop and think before risking his neck? Her love for him went through her like a knife, and she gritted her teeth to hold back the wild cry.

I care!

Five

"Are you going to invite me to move in here with you?" he asked bluntly a while later as they moved away from the small table in her kitchen.

Katrina had her back to him, and she was glad of that. She went to one of the wide windows and stood gazing out on the huge park spread out below. After a moment, infusing her voice with dryness, she said, "Are you going to wait for an invitation?"

"No."

"I didn't think so."

"You don't have to tell me my manners are rotten." There was a pause, and then he moved up behind her and slid his arms around her, pulling her back against him. And his voice was no longer amused when he said, "Ask me to stay, Trina."

She wondered vaguely if there would ever come a time when she didn't go weak at his simplest touch, and knew the answer. Some last vestige of pride made her voice light. "I suppose it would be stupid to keep your room when it isn't needed. And Hagen won't be surprised; I hear he's come to expect his agents to get involved with women."

"Damn Hagen." Skye turned her around, his hands hard on her shoulders. "Are you saying you don't want me here?"

She gazed up into his intense violet eyes, again baffled by the searching look they contained. Still clinging to her shred of dignity, she managed a laugh. "You know the truth of that, and why should I deny it? Don't worry, though, Skye. This passion of ours is too powerful to last very long. It'll burn itself out quite soon, I expect."

His mouth tightened. "Do you?"

Katrina smiled easily, the outward calm hiding her desperate inner struggle to hold on to something she could be left with when he was gone. Even if it would only be pride. "Naturally. Any fire dies once the fuel is gone. Without love, passion doesn't last." She winced when his hands tightened.

"So wise," he mocked her harshly. "Experience, Trina?"

Katrina felt a flicker of pain even though she was too familiar by now with his suspicious nature to be much hurt by it. "I told you there hasn't been anyone else."

"And I believed you. I wonder if I should have."

She gazed at him steadily. "That's up to you."

His hands lifted to her face as they so often did, holding her still for his searching scrutiny as if she were trying to escape him. "Where do you go?" he muttered.

She blinked, but couldn't answer the question even if she'd understood it. He kissed her before she could speak, his mouth hot and demanding. Katrina had been conscious of a languid physical weariness until then, but at the first touch of his lips sharp energy went through her like a jolt of electricity and her body came alive. She felt it all over, her breasts swelling, nipples tightening, a burst of heat deep in her belly, and her legs went weak and began trembling.

In an abrupt movement Skye ended the kiss, raising his head and staring down at her. His nostrils were flaring in a look that was almost savage, and when he released her and stepped back, his vivid eyes raked her body in a hard appraisal.

Katrina knew that her thin terry robe hid little, that her body's response to him was obvious. She put out a hand to the window frame to steady herself, looking at him with helpless longing. Did his hard face soften? She couldn't be sure.

"Now ask me to stay," he ordered in a dark and velvety voice.

"Stay." It was less a question than a plea, and her voice was almost inaudible, shaking. He could, she thought dimly, have the triumph if he wanted it.

Skye lifted one hand and cupped her cheek briefly. "I'll go and get my things." He turned away from her and, without bothering to put on shoes or a shirt, left her suite.

She stood where she was for a long moment. It was odd, she thought, but he hadn't seemed triumphant at her total inability to withstand him. Satisfied, yes, but mixed with that very male complacency had been something else, something she couldn't identify. Hurt? But that didn't make sense . . . unless he was beginning to care for her.

Katrina felt her heart almost stop. Was it possible? He was too complex to read easily; despite his quick temper and seemingly volatile mood swings, she knew that much of Skye lay beneath his compelling surface. Six years before he had been quick to voice his love, even impetuous in his words and actions, sweeping her along on an irresistible tide. But this older, more complicated man, she thought, was far more guarded and wary than he had been then. She had hurt him badly once, and even if she had somehow managed to touch his heart this time, he wouldn't be quick to admit it.

The realization gave Katrina a surge of hope, until she remembered what he had said to her only days before.

I did everything I could to forget you. Everything. But nothing worked, and I hated myself for that. You've been my own personal demon for six years, Katrina, locked inside me too deeply to be torn out.

Her hope faded. He had talked of obsession, she thought, not love. And he had not said or done anything since then to make those words meaningless. He had asked for a second chance, yes, and had bided his time with unusual patience. And he was clearly determined to make certain she couldn't ignore her own need for him. But no word of caring had passed his lips, and he had neither made promises nor asked for any.

I hated myself for that.

Could she ever be anything to him except an obsessive need he was bent on ridding himself of?

Katrina shook off the painful question and went slowly into her bedroom. She remade the bed with fresh linens and picked up the clothing still lying haphazardly on the floor. His shirt smelled of him, faintly musky and she wanted to bury her face in it.

Idiot. The inner scorn was unreal, and she knew it. She felt greedy in her love, desperate to take everything she could, to store memories in her mind and heart. Grimly she hung on to the thread of pride, determined to survive this if she could.

She changed into shorts and a thin blouse, then called down to have the room service cart taken away. It was a momentary temptation to ask to have her kitchen stocked, a luxury provided by the hotel that she had rarely taken advantage of, but the mental images that evoked made her resist. She and Skye weren't living together, she reminded herself fiercely. They weren't married. He was just staying in her suite for the duration of his assignment. Period. And she refused to be coy, to paint an illusion of domesticity by pandering to a little-woman-in-the-kitchen image.

A sudden memory brought her sense of humor to the rescue before she could get bogged down in self-pity. She wouldn't have been in the kitchen anyway. Unless he had forgotten more in six years than she had learned, Skye was a much better cook than she was.

She wandered around restlessly for a while after the room service waiter left. Then an abrupt thought sent her to the telephone, and she called the hotel's switchboard. "Megan, if there are any calls for Mr. Prescott, put them through to this number, will you?"

"Sure, Katrina." Megan giggled suddenly. "As a matter of fact, he already called me about that. Some women have all the luck!"

Katrina, who had kept her voice calm and dignified, cleared her throat and said, "Well, thanks, Megan," and quickly hung up. She sat staring at the phone, uncertain if she was amused or annoyed by Skye's swift action. Possession, she wondered, or professionalism? Had he been determined to alert the entire hotel via the talkative switchboard operator that he had moved in, or had he taken that step simply out of a good agent's precaution?

Ten minutes later, watching as he methodically unpacked in her bedroom, she had to know. "I thought Hagen might try to call you, so I phoned the switchboard. It seems you had the same thought. Megan all but congratulated me."

He straightened with his shaving kit in his hand and turned toward the bathroom, saying, "You're a fallen woman now."

Katrina stared after him, irritated by the satisfaction in his calm voice. She went to her dresser and began shifting some of her clothing to make room for his. "You didn't have to shout it to the whole place," she muttered.

Coming back into the bedroom, he patted her on the fanny as he passed. "No?"

She glared at his reflection in the mirror for a moment, but his quick smile disarmed her. He was in a better mood than he had been, she realized, and wondered if she'd ever fathom him. "No," she returned, but in a milder voice. "It may interest you to know that it's a well-known fact I don't sleep with guests, much less when they haven't been here a week."

He shrugged, but he was still smiling. "Bets have been on for two days now. I just thought somebody should win the kitty."

This time Katrina turned around to stare at him rather than at his reflection. "What?"

"Sure." His eyes were gleaming with amusement. "I wasn't supposed to know, but Dane told me about it yesterday. One of the room service waiters saw him practicing a crooked deal and asked if he liked betting pools. By the way, the odds were running strongly in my favor."

She didn't know whether to swear or laugh. "Are

you telling me that the staff has been betting on your chances of getting me into bed?"

"Yes. And they must have seen something I didn't; until this morning, I was almost ready to bet against me."

Katrina bit her lip, staring at him, then suddenly laughed. "Would you like to wager that Gigi didn't start it?"

Skye was looking at her intently, a different, softer smile playing around his firm lips. "No. Dane taught me long ago never to bet against a sure thing."

Without having noticed either her own laugh or his reaction to it, she shook her head and stepped over to pick up a pile of his shirts lying on the bed. "I'll have to ask Gigi who won," she said dryly. "It should be interesting."

He watched her place the shirts in a drawer, conscious of a deep surge of satisfaction. His shirts lying beside a stack of her T-shirts, his shaving gear set firmly among her perfumes and bath soaps. He had forced her to accept his presence here, and he damned well meant to put down roots and make sure she realized it. If he had to shake her loose from that secret place inside her head a dozen times a day, he'd do it.

And it wasn't just passion that made her unable to hide from him, though that was a surefire method and one he was prepared to use ruthlessly. Temper did it as well. She had been annoyed by his presumptuous order to have his calls routed to her number; her lovely eyes had flickered with irritation and there had been a definite snap in her voice. She had laughed, too, reluctantly amused by the knowledge that the hotel's staff had placed bets on the state of her virtue.

She had *laughed*.

Skye reached out suddenly and pulled her into his arms, smiling down at her when her arms went instantly around his neck. "Why did you get dressed?" he asked.

Katrina flushed slightly and cleared her throat. "Well, I felt a bit ridiculous wearing my robe in the middle of the afternoon," she explained.

"I should hope you would." He began exploring the soft flesh of her throat. "You'd better wear nothing at all."

She caught her breath. "Is that an order?"

"Yes," he said, unbuttoning her blouse with deliberation.

Katrina thought vaguely about telling him he couldn't order her around, but it didn't seem very important. And when his big hands slid inside her opened blouse, she forgot to think at all.

It was after midnight when Skye eased from the bed and dressed silently without turning on the lights. He was reluctant to leave Katrina even for a couple of hours, but after spending all day and half the night with her, his professional responsibilities were beginning to nag at him.

He had decided on the Ferris wheel: it was time to set the stage and prepare it for Hagen's inspection.

He had left his briefcase by the door, and picked it up on his way out. The hotel was peaceful, though there were still people stirring in the lobby, and he took care to make his exit unobtrusive. Dressed in the dark clothing he wore habitually, even when he wasn't skulking at night, Skye moved away from the hotel building, avoiding lighted paths. There was a locked gate between the hotel grounds and the park entrance; he had a key and used it swiftly.

Fifteen minutes later he was kneeling beside the lowest car of the Ferris wheel. The lack of bright light didn't hinder him since he had excellent night vision, and he quickly got his briefcase opened. He started to reach into the case and then froze, all his senses flaring. He had heard nothing, but—

He relaxed suddenly. In a low voice he said, "What're you doing out here?"

"Came to find you, of course. I knew you'd be out here tonight, since you'd settled on the Ferris wheel." Dane materialized out of the darkness and approached his brother. It was rather startling that he had been practically invisible until choosing to show himself, because he was wearing light-colored slacks and a white shirt that should have made him hard to miss. But Skye wasn't surprised by the seeming wizardry.

He had himself adopted dark colors largely because he lacked his brother's peculiar ability to seem to vanish into the darkness or the woodwork when he chose. Dane had explained the puzzle by talking about the difference between them. *You're like neon, and if there's an off switch, you haven't found it.*

After Skye had contrasted his brother's utterly tranquil surface with his own impatience and restlessness, he admitted to himself that Dane was probably right. Years of discipline had given Dane the ability to cloak his own nature, but Skye had never gotten the knack of that and doubted he ever would.

Now, as his brother knelt beside him, Skye reached into the briefcase and withdrew a neat square of malleable material. "Why were you looking for me?" he asked.

"Are you sure that stuff's inert?" Dane countered, watching with a wary gaze as Skye's long fingers began shaping the material.

Skye sent him a brief smile. "Modeling clay, but it looks like the real thing. If Hagen doesn't take it into his head to get an analysis, it'll pass muster. You didn't answer me."

"Ummm. You were a bit on edge this morning."

Skye swore softly. "I thought so."

"They have a vested interest in this caper," Dane pointed out dryly. "More than either of us, as a matter of fact. Our acquaintance with Hagen is fairly recent, but he's been meddling in their lives for a couple of years now. Raven just asked if I'd find out what was bothering you."

Skye set the clay aside and reached into his pocket for a Swiss Army knife. He drew out the screwdriver blade and began loosening a metal panel under the seat of a car.

"No answer?" Dane asked quietly.

"You know the answer." Skye's voice was curt. "And talking about it won't change anything."

"Cut it out," Dane ordered in a tone that matched his brother's. "I let you get away with silence six years ago because I hadn't been in love myself and didn't understand. In retrospect, it was a stupid decision on my part. You can tell me to go to hell if you want, but I'll be damned if I'll stand by *this* time and watch you tear yourself apart."

"That won't happen again." Skye sat back on his heels suddenly, his hands going still, and the ragged edge of strain showed in his voice. "At least I hope—dammit, I don't know. I just don't know." He laughed shortly. "I moved into her suite this afternoon."

"Is that as promising as it sounds?"

"No. I more or less forced her into it."

Remembering the temper he had seen in her flash-ing amber eyes, Dane said slowly, "I wouldn't have thought that lady could be pushed very far against her will."

"You've met her?" Skye said, not much surprised.

"By accident, the other day. She said that you and I were very different, and it wasn't a question."

Skye laughed again, and again the sound held no humor.

Dane hesitated, then said, "If you've been doing your talented impersonation of a bundle of dyna-mite, it's no wonder the lady's a bit wary." When his brother said nothing, Dane shook his head. "Are you giving her room to breathe, Skye?"

Skye began working on the Ferris wheel car again, his head bent. "I'm trying."

The mumbled answer made Dane's mouth twist in wry understanding. Skye was of course being his usual impatient, overpowering self, and Dane knew his brother's nature too well to try to change it at this late date. "Scars from the past getting in the way?" he asked instead.

"She says she doesn't blame me for what hap-pened in Germany." Skye removed the last screw from the metal panel, then carefully removed the panel and uncovered a small empty compartment beneath the car's seat.

"Do you believe that?"

"I don't know. I didn't trust her then, not when it counted, and she doesn't trust me now."

Dane was silent for a few moments, watching as his brother continued setting the stage for an at-tempted assassination. The darkness was no more a hindrance to Skye's quick, economical movements than it was to Dane's observation of his brother's closed face; they both possessed catlike night vision.

"Doesn't trust you how?" Dane asked finally, reflecting silently that this was like pulling teeth. "She's afraid you'll believe the worst of her again?"

"No. She's afraid I'll hurt her. I can see it in her eyes." Skye reached into the open compartment beneath the car's seat and began molding the clay into one corner.

Dane, who had been forced to cope with something similar in his own courtship, knew there was no simple answer for that one. "So what're you going to do about it?"

"Convince her she's wrong, if I can." Abruptly Skye added, "If it comes to that, maybe she isn't wrong. I've already hurt her, and I will again. God knows I don't mean to, but when has that ever stopped me."

"If you'd only *think* first," Dane said, and it held the sound of an old refrain.

"Teach me that, will you?" Skye requested with a thread of humor in his voice.

"Maybe Katrina can; I gave up a long time ago."

Skye laughed, and determinedly changed the subject. "Given the setup, it should be a remote-controlled detonation rather than a timer, don't you think?"

"I'd say so. Where will our assassin be lurking?"

His hands were once more busy preparing the lump of "explosive" for a remote detonation, but Skye nodded toward the nearest building, which was an elaborate fun house. "I'm going to suggest the roof of the fun house. There's a partially concealed ladder for a quick exit, and a clear field of vision."

Dane was frowning. "Makes sense. Now, how do you propose to handle the factor of random chance?"

"You mean making certain the governor is seated

in this particular car?" Skye chuckled. "I'm going to let Hagen worry about that one. It'll occupy his mind."

"Is there a solution?" Dane asked politely.

"God knows."

Dane couldn't help but laugh. "An accomplice?" he suggested.

"After he lost his terrorist group, Adrian became a loner," Skye reminded his brother. "We'll let random chance be a puzzle for Hagen. It won't go as far as getting the governor on the ride anyway. If our choreography is by the numbers, our assassin will be standing handcuffed in front of Hagen long before the crucial moment." He was busy replacing the metal cover.

A few minutes later Dane got to his feet as Skye closed the briefcase and rose. He respected his brother's privacy, and was perfectly aware that Skye's edginess earlier in the day had been largely a physical strain due to his enforced patience. Still, Skye was hardly relaxed now, and Dane knew he was tied into emotional knots because of Katrina.

So, as they walked back toward the hotel, he brought the subject up one last time. "Give her time, Skye," he advised softly. "You came back into her life less than a week ago; let her get used to the idea." He sent his brother a sudden grin. "I know you're convinced you could move the earth with a lever and someplace to stand, but it takes two to build a bond."

Skye thought about that later as he slipped into Katrina's suite and made his way to the bedroom. In the dark silence of the room he could hear her soft breathing, deep and even in sleep. As always, he could feel his body respond to her nearness and the thought of her with instant heat and need. These explosive emotions caught at his breath and his heart, clouding his mind until he was aware of nothing but his own driven urgency.

He stripped away his clothing rapidly and slid beneath the covers beside her. She was unaware of him in sleep, and he couldn't stand that; he wanted her aware of him all the time, just as he was always aware of her. It took two to build a bond, Dane had said, and the only certainty Skye had was that the desire between him and Katrina was a bond. She had told him with a steady voice and wary eyes that what was between them would soon burn itself out; he meant to prove to her how wrong she was about that.

He drew her slender, naked body into his arms and kissed her slightly parted lips, the sweet taste of her going to his head like raw brandy. She was warm and pliant, her flesh satin beneath the searching touch of his hands. She purred sleepily and cuddled closer, and that unconscious trust yanked a low groan from his very depths.

Dear Lord, he wanted her! He wanted to make himself a part of her until she could never escape him even in her most deeply buried thoughts, until she could never hide from him again. "Trina," he muttered, only half conscious of the jagged need in his own voice.

Her eyes fluttered open and her arms lifted lazily to his neck as he rose above her. "Again?" Her voice was throaty and wondering, and quick, passionate excitement flickered in her beautiful amber eyes.

"Again," he whispered, watching her face as he eased into her slowly. Her body accepted him instantly, completely, and he shuddered in stark pleasure as her tight heat surrounded him. Burying his face in the wild silk of her hair, he uttered thickly, "Again . . . and again . . ."

He couldn't move slowly now, his body responding to her sensuous grasp with lightning intensity and out of his control. The hunger he felt was ravenous, consuming, as if his very survival depended on this compulsive joining.

Katrina held on to him helplessly, no longer surprised by her body's instantaneous desire for him. Even just barely awake she was on fire for him, tension building in her with the force of a storm trapped under glass. He was moving inside her with compelling power, his big body above her like the vast shadow of some bird of prey, holding her trapped in a suspension greater than terror.

I love you. Her lips moved to shape the words she thought he wouldn't want to hear, her hands gripping his shoulders as her body wildly returned the slamming force of his. It was insanity, what he made her feel, a sweet madness she had no hope of controlling. All she could do was give way to the domination of it. From her throat came winging sounds like the sharp cries of some primitive creature, and she was unaware of the hot tears escaping from her closed eyes.

She was blind and deaf to everything except the sudden explosion of ecstasy that shattered her senses, and she could only hold him with what strength was left to her as his powerful body shuddered in a violent release.

Katrina returned to earth gradually, aware first of the weight of his body. She didn't want him to move, and some dim instinct told her it was because, in these lingering, peaceful moments after lovemaking, he was as vulnerable as she was, as trapped as she was.

Skye raised himself slowly on his elbows, the muscles of his arms quivering slightly. Even in the darkness she could see the luminous force of his eyes and the rough charm of his crooked smile. Then the smile died as his thumb brushed the wet skin near her temple.

"Tears?" His voice was low. "Did I hurt you?"

"No," she said.

"I don't want to hurt you, sweetheart." He hesitated, then said huskily, "I lose control when I'm with you. But if I've hurt you, tell me."

She lifted her head from the pillow and kissed his hard shoulder. "You haven't." And before he could probe to discover the source of her tears, she sacrificed a bit of pride to observe wryly, "I haven't exactly been passive myself."

"No, you haven't." He kissed her with unusual gentleness, as if he realized the cost of that admission. "I thought you had fire years ago, but I could never find it. It drove me half crazy. I should have realized you were too young then."

Katrina wasn't about to tell him that it wasn't a woman's body but a woman's love that had sparked that fire. She resisted the urge to protest when his weight left her, and cuddled close when he drew her firmly into his arms. It had given her a tinge of hope at first, this habit he had of holding her even after sleep claimed him. But then she had reminded herself that he was an extremely sensual man, and that it was no doubt his practice with all his bedmates.

It hurt.

He lost control with her, yes, but she had no way of knowing if that was unusual for him. The stoic voice in her head reminded her that he was by nature impatient and impetuous; given the enormous life force his big body held, she'd be a fool not to believe that sex had always been a release of sheer energy for him.

His arms tightened around her suddenly. "What is it?"

She wondered if he was beginning to read her mind, or if she had made some sound of pain. "Nothing. I was just wondering—" She broke off, fighting the urge to ask him.

"Wondering what?"

"It doesn't matter."

"Tell me."

Katrina cast the answer around in her mind. "Oh, just about you and Dane. You said years ago that he was your partner, and he's here now. So I was wondering about that."

Skye was silent for a moment, and then he shifted position, removing one arm from around her and propping his head on his hand so that he could look down at her. She realized vaguely that he always did that, watched her while he talked to her as if he were looking for something. And she had no doubt he could see her more clearly than she could see him; she couldn't hide from his vivid eyes in the darkness.

"We've been partners for ten years," he told her.

Katrina, a trained agent, could see the possibilities. "Did you use your . . . your uniqueness?"

He nodded slightly. "It was always our edge. We worked all over the world at first, but after Germany . . ."

"I ruined it for you," she said in a low voice.

The arm across her waist tightened. "Not really," he told her in a considering tone. "I'd been using my real name, but they didn't have a photograph of me.

The chances were good that I could have remained effective in Europe. But Dane and I were approached by a man who headed a domestic intelligence operation, and the offer was a good one. We were ready for a change."

"And no one knew you were twins?"

"Just Daniel. Dane had already developed an international reputation as a gambler, so we made his the public persona."

She saw his mouth twist suddenly, and felt a pang as she began to understand. "You were the one in the shadows?"

"Yes." His voice roughened. "It's where I wanted to be, hiding in the dark."

Like a wounded animal, she thought, and the pang was sharper this time. She made herself lie quietly even though she wanted to throw her arms around his neck, to comfort him somehow even though she found it hard to believe that anything could have done that to him. "Because . . . of Germany?"

"Does that surprise you?" He was very still, his gaze fixed intently on her face.

Katrina couldn't begin to read his expression in the darkness, and his steady voice gave her no clue to his thoughts or feelings. "Yes," she said finally, honestly.

"Why?" he rapped out.

"You're so strong," she said simply.

After a moment Skye eased back down at her side and used both arms to pull her closer. "Am I?" he asked in an odd tone, then gave the ghost of a laugh. "We'd better get some sleep."

Katrina didn't know what to make of those words. But, as she drifted off to sleep, the stark thought in her mind was that if she had hurt him that badly, he would never be able to love her again.

Skye woke before dawn, instantly aware Katrina wasn't with him. He reached out and turned on the lamp on her nightstand just as the bathroom door opened and she came out fully dressed. He sat up slowly, looking at her. She was ready for work, her royal blue silk dress elegant, her fiery hair tamed in a braided coronet. She looked beautiful and controlled and aloof.

"I'm sorry, I didn't mean to wake you," she said.

Even her voice was distant, he thought, and held a hand out to her. She hesitated, then came to the bed and didn't resist when he pulled her down so that she was sitting on the edge of the bed near his hips. He kissed her, holding her tightly in his arms until the faint stiffness left her and she melted against him with a smothered little sound. And when he raised his head at last, her eyes flickered and her lips were parted, softened and slightly swollen.

"Good morning," he said.

Katrina blinked at him. She felt a little wild for a moment, thinking that a greeting like his could easily make a woman useless for the rest of the day. Then she cleared her throat. "Good morning. I thought you should rest."

His lips quirked, and quick laughter gleamed in his eye. "Oh? Did I give you that impression?"

Realizing how that had sounded, Katrina flushed and got determinedly to her feet. "No," she admitted, her mouth going dry when he cast off the covers and slid from the bed. No matter how many times she saw his muscled body, she always felt an instant sense of surprise and wonder at the stark male beauty of him.

"I don't seem to be very tired," he decided.

Her gaze lifted hastily to meet his, and she cleared her throat again. "No," she agreed.

He tipped her chin up and kissed her again, this time lightly. "You usually have breakfast in the restaurant, don't you? Wait for me, and I'll go down with you."

Katrina didn't bother to voice an agreement, knowing he'd take it for granted. She wandered out into the den to wait while he showered and shaved, trying to piece back together the control he had shattered so easily.

So easily . . .

Six

"The human element," Hagen said in disgust, pacing the room and working himself into a fine state.

Gigi, watching with an elbow propped on her desk and her delicate chin resting in her cupped palm, said sympathetically, "It is most disheartening, I'm sure."

Disregarding the interpolation, Hagen continued to pace magnificently. "I knew it the moment he caught sight of her in the lobby. We're on the point of capturing an assassin and terrorist who has successfully eluded the combined law enforcement and intelligence agencies of the *world* for years, and Skye Prescott takes one look at a woman and goes to pieces. A trained, experienced agent, mind you, and a man I would have said could have dispatched Adrian with his bare hands."

In a reflective and somewhat dissatisfied tone, Gigi offered, "Not to pieces, not quite that." She sighed before attempting to redirect Hagen's thoughts. "You said Skye had found the explosives placed by Adrian, so he is obviously thinking of why you brought him here."

Hagen wasn't mollified. "He wasn't thinking at all once he caught sight of your Katrina. Send her away, Gigi!"

"No."

He stopped pacing, setting his palms on her desk and leaning toward her. In a voice of awful authority he said, "You must send her away."

Unimpressed and even a little amused, Gigi retorted, "It would be better for your blood pressure, Hagen, if you could bring yourself to realize that you do not command me. I will not send Katrina away. And if you were as wise about human nature as you claim to be about virtually everything else, you would know that Skye wouldn't be much good to you if I did."

Hagen stared at her for a moment, his blue eyes steely. Then he moved to her visitor's chair and sat down, heaving a gusty sigh. "I suppose not," he said unexpectedly.

Gigi blinked, then smiled.

Seeing her expression, he said testily, "I am not such a fool as you seem to believe!"

"I have never thought you a fool," she said definitely. "Egotistical, selfish, manipulative, arrogant, secretive, and always ruthless—but never a fool."

This measured and masterly description of his character brought a gleam to Hagen's eyes. "And I've never thought you a fool, my dear."

"No," she agreed, adding sweetly, "merely a lump of clay awaiting a molding hand."

He winced. "If I ever believed that," he muttered, "you rid me of the notion years ago."

"Not completely." Her voice was dry. "You continue to behave, in the face of all evidence to the contrary, as if you can bend me to your will."

Hagen eyed her speculatively. "I've never been able to do that, have I, my dear?"

"No. And you never shall." She watched his face and believed that for the first time he had accepted the truth. She saw something else as well, though no hint of that knowledge showed on her face. Skye, she thought, was not the only hard and capable agent who had allowed a woman to distract him from professional thoughts.

Hagen had forgotten all about Adrian.

The clowns of Fantasyland tended to wander all over the park, so it wasn't very surprising that one of them stood near a docked riverboat in the section called Seafaring Days and talked to an antebellum gambler. But more than one passing visitor stifled a laugh, mostly because the happy clown was busy consuming, under the fascinated eye of the gambler, a foot-long hot dog that seemed to have *everything* on it.

"Want a bite?" she invited cheerfully.

Dane winced. "Thank you, but no. My mind balks, to say nothing of my stomach. Is that black stuff caviar?"

"Uh-huh."

"On a hot dog?"

A faintly startled look refused to be hidden beneath her happy clown's makeup. "That is strange, isn't it? I've been putting it on everything lately."

Dane's firm mouth twitched. "A very extravagant craving," he noted politely.

Her eyes gleamed at him. "You've got to learn how to be an indulgent husband. After I ordered a jar from room service and put some on waffles, Josh just bought a case of the stuff and put it in the refrigerator in our room. I left him there a little while ago taking care of some business calls, and he didn't say a word when I got a jar out and put it in my money belt." She indicated the belt meant to hold the proceeds from her balloon sales, explaining, "I knew the hot dog vendor wouldn't have caviar."

He watched her finish the hot dog with undiminished enjoyment, shaking his head, then said, "I hope you'll pardon my inexperience in these matters, but should you be out here in this heat?"

Raven crumpled up her napkin and tossed it accurately into a nearby trash can. Dryly she told him, "The days of ladies in interesting conditions being waited on hand and foot are long past, pal—though Josh would, if I'd let him. I'm fine, believe me. Aside from my odd cravings, that is."

"If you say so."

He seemed a bit doubtful, and Raven couldn't help grinning. She had never in her life been treated like a frail flower, even by Josh, who openly adored her; pregnancy clearly changed all that, and it fascinated her. This "interesting condition" of hers was giving her a whole new perspective on the mysterious instincts of the male, and she was enjoying it. Being Raven, she explored the matter curiously.

"I realize that impending fatherhood must be as unnerving as impending motherhood," she said to Dane, "but what is it that makes you men go all to pieces about it? Josh was fine when we first found out, but the next morning at breakfast he suddenly went white as a sheet. He said it had just hit him."

Dane eyed her thoughtfully. "I can't speak from experience, but I think that *unnerving* is the wrong word. *Terrifying* is probably closer to the mark."

Raven considered that. "Well, I'll admit that parenthood is a scary proposition. But you men—all of you, not just my darling husband—look at a pregnant women with the most amazing fascination."

"We can't do it, you see," Dane explained gravely.

Staring at him, she said bemusedly, "You know, I never really thought about it in quite that way. But women have been having babies for two million years; I'd have thought you men would have gotten used to it by now. Especially since science and Lamaze classes have pretty much robbed pregnancy of its mysteries."

Thoughtfully Dane said, "I imagine every man gets a shock when the matter becomes a personal one. Besides, you women are biologically designed to cope. There aren't any physical changes or hormonal influences on a man's emotions when he's about to become a father. He's exactly the same as he was before. I think most of us would choose to share the emotions of our wives, but the simple fact is that we can't feel the same, not really. We don't know what the kick of a baby feels like from inside, and we have nothing to compare it to. What we do feel is fascination, because the process is so alien to us despite all the knowledge available to us. Pregnancy is so amazing." He laughed suddenly. "And if Jenny ever asks me the same question, I'll probably be totally incoherent when I try to answer."

Raven was smiling. "Josh was. And he never is, you know." She shook her head in bemusement, then asked abruptly, "How's Skye?"

"I didn't think you came out here just to share your lunch," Dane said.

"It isn't simple professional interest." She looked at him seriously. "Once he came out of the dark and stopped being you, I could see the shadows still holding on to him. And shadows like his mean pain. You don't have to tell me that the two of you are as different as night and day, but you're both natural actors, very adept at hiding your feelings, and Skye's method is a shell as hard as granite."

"Not entirely a shell," Dane said reluctantly.

Raven nodded. "Yes, that's why I didn't go to him directly. He'll always be difficult only *some* of the time. And he's probably," she added in a thoughtful tone, "as obstinate as a mule."

Dane grinned. "Woman's intuition?"

She eyed him darkly. "No. Merely perception born of experience with a certain breed of men. Teddy calls them dragon slayers, and it's as good a word as any. You're one yourself, and don't try to deny it. Most of them hide steel cores under a layer of deceptively softer material. Josh is charming; Rafferty is lazy; Zach is soft-spoken and mild—though he doesn't hide the steel very well; Luc is charming; Kelsey is often absurd; Derek is calm. And you, pal, are the most tranquil man I've ever met. You hide the steel best of all. But it's there."

"And Skye?" Dane asked curiously.

Raven smiled faintly. "He doesn't even try to hide it. Skye is hard and tough, impatient and reckless, and so intense he's pretty well bound to go off the deep end no matter what emotion he's coping with. I'd guess he's about as easily pushed as a mountain and about that easy to lead, and if he ever loves a woman he'll be putty in her hands."

Dane's eyes gleamed. "You ought to be burned at the stake," he observed.

She looked modest. "Just a natural talent." Then she sobered and said, "But that doesn't really help me in knowing if he's all right. Katrina is a stranger to me, so I can't begin to guess how she's coping with the kind of intensity that would unnerve most women from ten feet away."

Dane wasn't surprised Raven knew Katrina's name, even though he hadn't told her. She had an uncanny knack of finding out things whenever her curiosity was aroused. And he wasn't very surprised by her perceptive analysis of Skye's character; she had known Skye as long as she'd known him, and he didn't doubt that once their secret had been disclosed, she had very accurately pinpointed those occasions during the past years when Dane had actually been Skye.

"How is she coping?" she asked him bluntly.

Dane frowned "I haven't seen enough of her to know. I don't think Skye's sure either."

Raven stared at him for a moment. "Shadows. Pain. A dark and stormy past?"

He was startled by that. "You are a witch!"

"No. But dragon slayers tend to love only once, and be rather violent about it. I watched Skye with Hagen at the Ferris wheel a little while ago, and the pain was still there. Since Katrina hasn't cured him of it, she must have caused it. Makes sense."

"They got a second chance," Dane said, tacitly confirming her guess.

"I hope they make it this time," said Raven, who knew when to stop prying. Then, dryly, she added, "I suppose we should have known that any caper involving Hagen would spawn a romance. You might want to tell Skye that so far, our inadvertent cupid is batting a thousand."

"I'll tell him." Dane chuckled suddenly. "Although, according to Skye, there may very well be a second romance in the offing."

"Oh? Whose?"

"Hagen's."

Raven blinked. "You're kidding."

"Nope. It appears that Hagen and Gigi aren't quite the bitter enemies rumor has it they are. All sound and a fury that isn't anger, if you get what I mean.

And I happen to know that the staff of the hotel has two betting pools going. One concerned Skye and Katrina; the second, I hear, has been going on since the first time Hagen visited Gigi here years ago. And the odds have shortened. As of this morning, over half the hotel staff believes that Gigi will get him to the altar—this time."

A smile of unholy amusement slowly matched the clown's grin on Raven's face. "Hoisted by his own petard! Ohhh! It's priceless! Wait until Josh hears."

Enjoying her delight, Dane nonetheless cautioned, "It isn't a sure thing, you know. They've known each other for twenty years, and the staff seems to think Gigi's been trying to catch him for the last ten."

Raven's smile remained, but the light in her eyes became speculative. "I wonder . . ."

Dane was a perceptive man and, moreover, had some experience with Raven's shrewd, intelligent mind. So he felt torn between amusement and fascination as he watched her bright eyes and realized an idea was forming in her brilliant mind. "What're you up to?" he demanded.

"I think I'll call Serena," Raven answered.

"Who?"

"Josh's sister. She has a wonderfully devious mind and great instincts about people."

After a moment Dane said, "Are we still talking about Hagen?"

"Yes. And his trip to the altar."

Dane would have been the first to admit that Raven knew her ex-boss far better than he did, but he also knew Hagen's reputation. "I wouldn't have thought he could be any more easily lead than Skye can," he ventured.

An irrepressible giggle escaped Raven. "Oh, he's very easily led, once you know how to do it. Just witness our present caper. And, in language you of all people will understand, we can't possibly lose this game. Aces are wild—and we're holding all of them."

As he watched her stroll away, Dane reflected that she was quite right. Between them, Raven and her friends had stacked the deck very neatly for this unusual poker match.

Hagen, master gamesman though he was, was about to lose to a hand full of aces.

Katrina should have realized, after the previous day, that Skye wasn't a man who allowed little things like schedules to interfere with his pleasures. It hadn't occurred to her, first because she was so accustomed to having a job with fixed hours, and second because he had appeared both to accept and respect her duties in the hotel, that was, until Friday.

She had managed to reconstruct her control after he'd shattered it this morning, and was working steadily at her desk when he came into her office just before lunch. The computer screen before her flickered with the swiftly moving data of the hotel's accounts, and she was concentrating fixedly.

Some part of her felt him come in, but she was able to keep most of her mind on the work, and that was something of a relief. Without looking up she said, "Did you show it to Hagen?" He had told her what he'd done this morning at breakfast and that he intended to take Hagen out there.

"Yes. He had me 'disarm' it but leave it there. He's now busy trying to outthink Adrian on the matter of random chance." Skye moved around the desk until he was beside her and bent to kiss the bare nape of her neck.

Katrina controlled a shiver and glared at the computer's inoffensive screen. "Just as you thought. What do you mean to do now?"

"Take you upstairs," he said, exploring the scented flesh beneath her right ear.

She had automatically hit the key that stopped the program she was running, but managed to hold her body stiff. "Skye, I have to do these accounts. It's the end of the month, and they have to be done today."

"Later," he dismissed her impatiently.

"It'll take all day, even with the computer. I'm not even planning on breaking for lunch."

He suddenly yanked her up from the chair and pulled her into his arms. "Then quit the damned job," he said in a voice that was little more than a growl.

Skye knew it was a mistake the moment the words left him. He had spoken without thinking as usual, and as usual it was because she was hiding from him. Her cool, elegant figure behind the desk inflamed him because she looked so damned untouchable, and her faintly absent tone made it worse. He could barely think when she was nearby; in fact, he had enraged Hagen by losing the thread of conversation as he watched her walk through the lobby over an hour before.

And his own loss of control was doubly galling because her control appeared so solid. She lost it in passion, and in anger, but it never deserted her for long. And as far as he could tell, a casual glance or touch from him never so much as rippled the smooth surface of her serenity. She was aloof except when she was in his arms. As cool and elusive as moonlight, as hot and bright as sunlight; the paradox of her maddened him.

He had thought that finding the fire in her would be enough, but he had discovered it wasn't. He wanted her to burn for him, always, the way he burned for her always. He hated everything that took her attention away from him for even an instant, and knowing his ferocity stemmed from his own insecurity about her feelings for him did nothing to change it.

"What?" she gasped now, staring up at him.

He gazed at her lovely face, and what he wanted to say was *I'm going crazy with wanting you; don't shut me out!* But, incurably graceless whenever strong emotions gripped him, he of course said the last thing he should have.

"I said quit the damned job," he repeated impatiently, and rapidly made bad worse. "You don't need to work. I'll take care of you."

Katrina shoved him away with unexpected strength, her amber eyes snapping. "Thanks, but no thanks," she said tightly. "I may be a fallen woman, as you so aptly put it, but I'll be *damned* if I'm a kept one!"

She wasn't composed now, but Skye was belatedly aware that this kind of fire was likely to burn more than his hands. He had never before seen her this angry, and even while he was busy cursing himself he couldn't help but be fascinated. "Oh, hell, I didn't mean—I'm sorry, Trina—God, you're beautiful," he interrupted himself to say intensely.

The impulsive comment didn't mollify her in the least. In fact, if she'd been angry before, she was furious now. "You may think my job is nothing, an inconvenience in your sex life, but you can think again," she snapped. "I won't drop everything when you whistle, and I sure as hell won't be tumbled into bed because you're in the mood for a quickie!"

He laughed, unable to help himself, as her innately gentle voice shaped the blunt words. If he had considered it, he would have been surprised that her burst of rage did nothing to spark his own ready temper; oddly enough, he felt no anger at all, but only a sheepish desire to make amends.

"Don't laugh at me!" she practically shouted.

"I'm not," he assured her hastily, reaching out for her and being held off when she shoved the chair between them. "Trina, I didn't mean it the way it sounded—"

"I don't care how you meant it," she snarled.

"Please, sweetheart—"

"Get out of *my* office," she ordered with a sudden and fiery dignity. She pushed the chair away and began shoving him toward the door.

Somewhat to his surprise, he found himself going. "Trina, for heaven's sake!"

"This hotel is filled with women," she told him fiercely. "Try whistling to one of *them*."

"But I don't want one of them," he protested, and winced when the door was slammed in his face. He stood staring at the unyielding wooden barrier, resisting a sudden urge to kick the thing as he heard the metallic click of the lock.

"Damn." He turned around, and felt a flush climb into his face as he saw Gigi.

She was standing with her arms folded, her face solemn but a demon of laughter in her eyes. In a dispassionate tone she said, "Anyone who could rouse Trina to a display of that magnitude must be a veritable fiend."

"You're a lot of help," he said in a disgruntled voice.

"You haven't asked for my help," she told him politely.

He stared at her for a moment. "Help."

With a faint smile she said instantly, "You have a certain amount of charm, even if it is a bit rusty from disuse. And though you aren't a gentle man, there is a great deal to be said for being a gentleman."

Skye stood still for a moment after she strolled away, then turned and headed purposefully for the lobby. One of the desk clerks giggled as he passed, and another gave him a somewhat awed look, both reactions telling him that at least part of Katrina's outburst had been overheard.

And that, he reflected ruefully, just might sink his ship for sure.

For a full ten minutes after she'd slammed and locked the door, Katrina was so angry she could barely think. Gradually, however, the inevitable let-down overcame her, and she sank into her chair to stare at the computer. Her head was pounding, and she felt both a mild astonishment at her anger and a sense of bafflement at Skye's words.

His demand that she quit her job seemed, on the surface at least, to have sprung from sheer sexual domination, and that was what had sparked her rage. She had been furious, and mixed with that had naturally been her own sense of hurt that he apparently thought so little of her work that he would order her to abandon it without hesitation.

But a certain amount of bitter experience reminded her now that he often spoke without stopping to consider the probable impact of his words, and that his innate impatience made him quick to demand what he wanted. And what had he wanted in those first moments after he'd come into her office?

Her.

He hadn't thought about her work at all, except as

something standing between the two of them. And, intolerant as always, he had simply taken the quickest and most direct route to getting what he wanted. Her job was in the way—so he wanted it shoved to one side. It wasn't important, and the added comment about taking care of her had just been an impatient, purely expedient rider along the lines of "Never mind. I'll take care of it."

"Arrogant so-and-so," she told the computer.

He *was* arrogant . . . but she wasn't surprised by it, and couldn't seem to get angry about it. She might just as well get angry at a comet for following its natural path. He hadn't meant to hurt or upset her, and it had probably never occurred to him that he would. And, to do him justice, he had instantly tried to apologize.

It was odd, she realized, but he hadn't gotten angry in return. He had been clearly intrigued by her temper, and he had laughed at her—No. Not *at* her, but at what she had said. Thinking about what she had said, she had to admit it sounded amusing in retrospect.

A knock at the door interrupted her thoughts, and she went to unlock it. Then she stepped back, startled, as one of the bellmen carried in a delicate crystal vase holding an enormous bouquet of long-stemmed red roses.

"Doesn't waste much time, does he?" the bellman observed cheerfully as he set the vase on her desk.

Two realizations struck Katrina then. One, that she lived in a goldfish bowl and, two, that Skye's impatience and temper weren't the only extravagant things about him. In the most dignified tone she could manage, she said, "Thank you, Dennis."

"There's a card," Dennis said with a wink, and then escaped before she could throw something at him.

Katrina eyed the offering for a moment, then plucked the card from among the blooms and retreated behind her desk. She sat down and opened the little envelope cautiously, not entirely certain what to expect.

I've forgotten how to whistle, but it doesn't matter. I want only you. I can't make pretty speeches about it; a starving man doesn't ask—he just grabs. I didn't mean to hurt you.

Thank heaven he wrote it himself, she thought vaguely, never doubting that the decisive, bold strokes of the pen were his. And what could a woman do with a man like Skye? A rough apology, blunt and without grace . . . and utterly disarming.

"Damn you," she murmured.

Katrina sat for a long time, her gaze almost blind. Then she turned off her computer and left her office. She didn't think about where she was going or what told her he'd be waiting for her, but she wasn't much surprised to find herself opening the door of her suite and going in. He wasn't in the den, but she went on into the bedroom. And he was there.

She held the card up briefly before putting it on the dresser. "You knew I'd come," she accused.

"No." Wearing only a pair of dark sweat pants and looking vibrantly male he came toward her slowly, "I hoped. But I wasn't sure."

"Dammit, you got me up here anyway!"

He smiled just a little, a crooked smile, and his eyes were luminous. "They say if you wish hard enough, you can make the wish come true."

Katrina cleared her throat, feeling the heat of his powerful body as he stood before her and stingingly aware that her body was responding instantly, as if he had reached out and enveloped it in his own intensity. "Is that what you did?" she managed to ask huskily.

"Yes." He reached up slowly and began unwinding her braid, tossing the pins carelessly aside and watching intently as fire flickered in the auburn strands that fell over her shoulders and curled wildly.

"You—you had no right to make that demand of me," she managed to say. "No right at all."

"I know." Though his voice contained a husky undertone, it was quiet and steady. He slipped around behind her, his hands smoothing the silk that covered her upper arms, rubbing slowly in a movement that was lazy and soothing.

"My job is important to me," she whispered, feeling her bones begin dissolving. He gently pushed her thick hair aside so that it fell forward over one shoulder, and she bowed her head instinctively when his warm lips touched the exposed nape of her neck.

"Of course it is," he whispered against her neck, his fingers dealing with the long row of buttons down her back. "I know that. You're a trained, experienced agent. You're also a hotel manager with responsibilities. I could never ask you to give up any part of what you are."

Katrina caught her breath as the silk dress slid down her body and pooled in a glimmering circle of blue around her feet. His hands were at her waist now, pulling her gently back against him, and she was trying to think long enough to get this matter understood between them. "Then why did you?"

"I wanted you," he said deeply. One of his hands lay on her stomach, fingers spread wide over the blue silk of her teddy, and his other hand slid slowly down her side to her thigh and began toying with the garter holding up her stocking. "I saw you walk across the lobby, and I couldn't think of anything else. You looked so cool and beautiful, as if you'd never gone crazy in my arms. I wanted you to go crazy again, to forget everything but me and wanting me."

His mouth was moving over her neck and shoulder, trailing fire. With her head still bowed, she looked dazedly at his powerful hand covering her middle, beautiful and starkly male, and watched the long fingers of his other hand expertly unfastening the snaps holding her stocking. She could feel his body hardening against her, his heat almost scorching her. Her eyes felt heavy, the lids half closing, and she was only vaguely aware that he had unfastened the other stocking and then the garter belt.

She swayed, and her hand came out to brace herself on his shoulder as he knelt beside her. He was smoothing the stockings down her legs, removing her shoes and the gossamer hose. When he stood up again, she turned naturally to him and would have gone eagerly into his arms if he'd let her.

But Skye held her away from him, his hands grasping her upper arms firmly. His brilliant eyes moved slowly over her body, then lifted to her face. "If I'd known you were wearing this sexy thing underneath your dress," he said thickly. "I would have locked the door of your office and taken you right there."

She gasped when he pulled her slowly to him, his words and the burning strength of his body making her feel naked despite the teddy. Her mouth opened brazenly under the almost bruising force of his lips, and she clung to him as he lifted her in his arms and carried her to the bed.

She wanted him. . . .

The desire he kindled in her mind and body was such a vast, overpowering, all-consuming thing that

Katrina never wanted gentleness from him, or patience, or even tenderness. She just wanted *him*. She didn't think in his arms; she could only feel with the simple, stunning pleasure of totally awakened senses. She became a wild thing, crazy with the desperate need for him, and no matter how primitive and forceful his passion was, she gloried in it.

The knowledge that he lost control with her, that she excited him as potently as he excited her, freed her to experience fully the unexpected depths of her own passions. She might have tried to hold back, even in bed with him, but his hunger and fierceness combined with her own love shattered her control so completely she couldn't have.

It wasn't even a matter of giving herself, but simply a matter of a possession that was mutual.

Her own blind fervor drove his desire higher; she knew that because he made no secret of it. If he couldn't make pretty speeches about his need, he charmed in a different, rougher way, his hoarse voice uttering raw words of stark necessity that seared her to her bones. And his hands on her, his beautiful hands that were hard without hurting, brought her body to life in a way she had never thought possible.

Katrina lost herself so utterly in the heat and frantic urgency of his passion that she thought she'd never find herself again. And some dim instinct told her he had marked her forever, inside where it wasn't visible to the naked eye. Deep inside her, where it burned like a brand on her soul.

The bedroom had been peaceful for some time when Katrina became aware of a guilty memory. The accounts. It was already the middle of the afternoon; she didn't stand a chance of finishing up by the end of the day even if she went back to work immediately. She was debating with herself as to whether Skye would protest her leaving him, when the sudden summons of the phone on her nightstand made the matter academic.

"Oh damn," Skye muttered in disgust, removing one arm from around her to reach for the pesky intruder. "What?" he growled into the receiver.

And Katrina, held closely beside him, didn't need the abrupt stiffening of his body to alert her, because she heard the hard voice of the caller almost as clearly as he did.

"Skye? He's loose."

Seven

"How the hell did that happen?" Skye bit out, releasing Katrina and sitting bolt upright. His expression was grim.

She sat up slowly beside him, still hearing the caller's voice clearly because it was so powerful, so distinct.

"I don't know yet, but I mean to find out," the caller promised darkly. "I just got a call from one of the agents; the other's in bad shape and needs to be taken to a hospital. It happened half an hour ago. Adrian didn't try to take the car, he simply vanished into the hills. I told Thompson to get his partner to a doctor and keep his mouth shut. In ten minutes I can be airborne with a squad of marshals."

"We can't have a manhunt out there, or we'll tip our hand for sure," Skye said flatly.

"It isn't a game anymore, Skye," Daniel Stuart, director of the FBI, said in a sharpened tone.

"You owe these people." Skye's voice was hard. "And you gave your word, Daniel."

"I can't have Adrian running loose down there!"

"He won't be for long." Skye threw back the sheet covering his naked body and swung his legs off the bed. "I'll get him."

"Alone? Skye, are you out of your mind?"

"I'm not alone. There's a small army here, one you'd love to get your hands on anytime, and they have a vested interest in capturing Adrian."

There was a pause, and then Daniel swore violently. "I don't like it—"

"You didn't like it when they made it possible for me to catch him the first time. Forget your marshals, Daniel. Bring only enough men to hold on to him. See you there." And he hung up the phone decisively.

Katrina knew that Adrian had been held in a remote house no more than ten miles from the park, and the thought of that killer loose on an unsuspecting countryside frightened her. But something else frightened her more, sending ice through her veins and tightening her throat until she could hardly speak.

Almost inaudibly she said, "You won't get the others, will you?"

Skye rose from the bed and began dressing. "There's no need. Adrian can't get far, not on foot. I'll be able to move faster if I go alone." He retrieved his gun from the top shelf of her closet, where he had put it the day before, and shrugged into the shoulder harness.

"I'm going with you." Katrina said, throwing off the covers and sliding from the bed. She went to the dresser and began hauling out clothing.

"No, you aren't," he said flatly, sliding his bare feet into moccasins and reaching into the closet for a thin Windbreaker.

"Skye!"

"Katrina, you aren't an experienced field agent trained to handle this kind of thing." He came to stand before her suddenly, one hand lifting to frame her face. His eyes were shuttered, his voice still harsh. "You'd only get in my way. Believe me, I know what I'm doing."

She stared up at him, holding the still-folded clothes to her naked breasts. In a wondering tone she said, "Dane was right. You do think you're made of iron, don't you?"

He gazed at her lovely, still face, aware that her catlike amber eyes held shock, that her slender body was rigid. In spite of the urgent need for him to get moving, he was fighting the urge to discover why she was looking at him with that expression of strange surprise. He didn't understand it. His own actions made perfect sense to him; Adrian had escaped, and he was going after him.

"I have to go," he said, ignoring her question and hearing the reluctance in his own voice.

She dropped the clothes she was holding and grabbed handfuls of his jacket. "Answer me!" she demanded.

Skye was trying to keep his attention off her naked body, and having little luck. The late afternoon sunlight filtered through the sheer curtains of the window, painting her body gold and lighting her wild hair with fire. He hated leaving her! "Of course I don't think I'm made of iron," he said finally, irritable because the question was unimportant.

"Then why are you going alone?" Her voice was fierce, her eyes burning. "Get Dane! Get *someone*!"

He forced patience into his voice. "I told you—I'll move faster alone. I've tracked Adrian before, and I know how his mind works." He bent his head and kissed her firmly, then pulled her hands loose from his jacket and stepped back.

"Don't," she said.

Skye turned away from her, surprised at the effort it took. And it wasn't, he realized, just because he could hardly stand to be out of her presence these days. It was something else, something on a deeper level—a wrenching tug inside him, as if some vital part of himself were irrevocably connected to her and resisted his leaving her. He had never felt anything like that before, and it disturbed him. "I'll be back," he muttered, and knew his promise was unvarnished truth.

He'd always return to her, no matter what stood in his way.

Katrina dressed in desperate haste, softly cursing her trembling fingers, trying to make her mind work. Dane, of course. He knew his brother best, he knew what she had only just seen clearly for herself. He had tried to warn her, but she hadn't listened, hadn't believed that a man with Skye's strength could ever need anyone else for any reason.

He needs someone to care about him, so he'll stop to think before risking his neck.

She had seen it for the first time, that unconscious, heedless inability in him to recognize the fact that he was made of flesh and blood. It had shocked her, because until then she hadn't known what Dane's warning had meant. But she knew now. She knew that Skye's very strength, the burning life force inside him, made him completely, unconsciously, reckless when it came to his own survival.

Katrina had fought for her survival, grimly and with all the will she could command. She had stoically endured interrogation techniques expressly designed to break the human mind and spirit, and had refused to be broken. She had faced her child-hood terror of small rooms and close places, reject-ing the mind-shattering horror of a nightmare come to life as she had stared at four bare gray walls in a three-by-five-foot cell. And she had emerged with a sure grip on her sanity to rebuild her life.

She knew how precious life was, and how vulnera-ble that life was to the vagaries of fate.

But Skye . . . He didn't know. Nature had given him a natural impatience and recklessness, and then had added both an unusual physical strength and an inner fire that burned with all the invincible heat of a crucible.

What had he said about Dane finding him months after he had left Germany? *I probably would have managed to get myself killed. God knows I was trying hard enough.*

His own life didn't matter very much to him. And it wasn't a defeatest thing, but simply a careless one; he never thought about it. He would always be largely indifferent to his own fate, she knew now. But his great strength and incredible life force had provided a kind of aura, a rare cloak of sheer luck, and he had survived despite his own hell-bent recklessness.

But luck was a capricious thing.

What Skye needed was, as Dane had warned, some-one who cared about him. He needed someone to love him so utterly that he became a part of that other life and, so, linked to it. Careless with his own existence, he would never be careless with another's, particularly if he loved as well.

Dane had been his balance, Katrina realized, re-membering the truth in what he had so lightly said. He had been Skye's center, his anchor. The more patient and cautious brother had held firmly to the bond between them, refusing to allow Skye to fling his life away without a thought. But Dane was married, his own heart claimed by the woman he loved, and though there wasn't less between the brothers, there was a difference. Skye was more alone, less connected.

And, as she raced from the hotel and through the park, Katrina promised herself fiercely that she would forge the bond he needed. She had been afraid to offer her love, but there was no room in her now for such insecurity. Skye's life meant more to her than her own, and she was prepared to fight with all the relentless will she could command to make certain he knew it.

He might not be able to love her, but he would never again be able to doubt that he was loved.

She drew up, breathless, a few yards from the docked riverboat. Dane was there, along with a lovely blonde who had to be his wife, as well as two other men, Derek and Kelsey, whom Katrina had met earlier while this operation was in the planning stages. All four were in casual clothes, having obviously changed from their costumes at the end of their shift.

And before she could even find the breath to speak, Dane was alert and aware. For the first time, she felt the force that he shared with his brother, saw it leaping at her out of his eyes as he instinctively probed.

She found her voice. "Adrian's escaped. Skye's gone after him."

"When?" Dane rapped out.

"Just as few minutes ago. Daniel Stuart called. One of the agents was badly hurt and the other one took him to the hospital. Adrian doesn't have a car; he's on foot somewhere in the hills. Skye wouldn't let Daniel bring in marshals; he said that all of you could recapture Adrian. But he meant to go alone, and he did."

Softly Derek said, "We have a chopper on the roof of the hotel. Would Skye—?"

Dane shook his head. "A skill neither of us has. He must have taken his car."

"Derek's a pilot," Kelsey offered, his pleasant face grim. "With a little luck Skye won't be more than a few minutes ahead of us."

"He's probably there already," Dane muttered, because one trait the brothers shared was a love of fast cars. He looked down at his wife, seeing her pallor and worried eyes. "Jenny— "

"I know," she said quickly, managing a reassuring smile. "Just be careful." She looked at Derek and said, "I'll tell Shannon and the others."

He nodded his thanks. All of them were conscious of the passing moments, and there was no time to stop and plan. No more than a couple of minutes after Katrina had found them, she was hurrying back across the park with the three men.

"I'm coming with you," she told them fiercely.

Kelsey opened his mouth, but Dane shook his head slightly at the other man and said, "Good" to her.

"There are a few guns stowed inside the chopper," Kelsey said instead. "Enough for us."

Katrina was still coldly afraid for Skye, but the three men she was with solidly inspired confidence. They were all big men, and though each would be formidable alone, in a group they were impressive as hell, she thought. She trusted Dane simply because he loved Skye, too, and because he shared with his brother that rare, enormous strength. Derek, blond and with serenely expressionless dark eyes in a hard, handsome face, was so calm and casually graceful that Katrina didn't doubt he knew his own strength to the last ounce. And then there was Kelsey, whose pleasant face and gray eyes concealed, she thought, the kind of danger that came from a very rough life.

She trusted them all, and they inspired confidence. But Skye was out there alone, trailing a soulless killer, and he didn't know that another heart was inextricably connected to his own.

Buckling her seat belt in the helicopter, she leaned forward to speak to Dane while Derek was checking over the craft's instruments. "You tried to warn me," she said jerkily, "but I didn't understand. If I had, maybe I could have stopped him. I'm sorry."

Dane half turned in the front seat to look back at her, and though his face was drawn, he was smiling faintly. "Don't blame yourself, Katrina. I certainly don't. And you probably couldn't have stopped him anyway. It may take a little practice before you're able to do that."

"Can you?" she asked him.

"No. I can't stop him. But you will be able to."

The roar of the helicopter as Derek started it put an end to the conversation, and Katrina sat back, conscious of hope surging inside her. Had Dane meant what she thought? She half closed her eyes as the helicopter lifted from the roof of the hotel, praying she'd get a chance to find out.

Skye left his car in the woods near the sprawling farmhouse and approached on foot, swift but with the instinctive caution of a wild animal. He doubted that Adrian had returned to the house once he'd escaped, but he had hunted the killer before and knew he was capable of just about anything.

No more than a minute served to convince him the house was deserted, and he slipped inside to take a quick look around. The place was peaceful and silent, but overturned and smashed furniture and a patch of blood drying on the living room carpet told of recent violence. Skye was about to leave, when he caught sight of a crumpled map on the floor beside the couch, and he bent to pick it up. A map of the area, he realized; he had seen a similar map when he and Daniel had decided on this place as the best available spot in which to hold Adrian captive.

Had the killer seen the map? Skye had to assume he had. And that Adrian had cannily spent his two weeks of incarceration trying to find out all he could about the area. Daniel's agents weren't stupid men, of course, but Skye knew only too well the boredom that inevitably led to guards relaxing after an uneventful passage of time.

Spreading the map out on the kitchen table, Skye studied it carefully, still holding his gun. Ten miles of wilderness all around the house, but . . . There was a long-abandoned coal mine nearby, clearly marked on the map. It had been a prosperous shaft in the past, but when explosives had broken into a natural artesian well, waters under pressure had flooded half the shaft. And, Skye remembered suddenly, that property had recently been surveyed again. Daniel had mentioned it while they had gone over the maps.

Skye marked the location of the mine in his memory and left the house, moving swiftly. He returned to his car briefly to get a flashlight from the glove compartment. Then he set out in the direction of the mine, and within fifty yards found signs that another man had also chosen this way. And Skye knew why.

Adrian was hoping to find explosives, either left there when the shaft was abandoned or brought more recently because the mine was due to be worked again. Even if armed—and Skye had to assume he was—the international terrorist and assassin felt naked without explosives. It was his single weakness, tactically speaking, and Skye had exploited that once before.

He would again.

Less than ten minutes later Derek came out of the farmhouse holding a large map. "This was on the kitchen table," he explained to the others. "Someone was looking at it."

Dane was frowning slightly, and then he turned suddenly and stared off to the west. "The mine. Daniel said there was a mine nearby."

About a mile away," Kelsey said, studying the map. "But why in God's name would Adrian go for it? If he heads cross-country, he'll hit a town sooner or later, even if he doesn't know the area. He could get some wheels and pretty much disappear. If he heads for the mine, he's got a lot of hellish terrain and no chance at all of making any time."

"Explosives," Dane said flatly.

"But he must be armed," Katrina objected in a voice she tried hard to hold steady. "And if he heard the helicopter, wouldn't he just run?"

Derek looked at her, his hard eyes softening as they took in her pale, taut features. "I doubt either of them heard the bird," he told her quietly. "We came in from the east, and between the dense forest and all these hills, the sound was probably muffled."

"And Adrian has a weakness when it comes to explosives," Dane said. "He's never long without them.

If he knows about the mine, he might have decided to take the chance."

She gazed at him blindly, then took a firmer grip on the automatic in her hand and said evenly, "Then we'd better try the mine. Anybody bring a flashlight?"

Kelsey was already striding toward the silent helicopter they had set down near the house. He caught up with them when they were about twenty yards from the house, carrying a big five-cell flashlight. He said, "If we have to go into that mine, we'll have to be careful with the light; anybody holding one is a target."

No one offered a comment.

Dane found the tracks left by his brother and Adrian about thirty yards farther along, and with their guess confirmed they were able to move faster. None of them was dressed for hiking, but although the area was thickly forested, the underbrush was sparse and the footing was fair. As Kelsey had observed, the terrain was hellish, but they all managed to move very swiftly.

It took almost half an hour for them to reach the dark, timber-shored opening in the side of a deceptively small hill. Katrina would have instantly gone forward and into the earthly maw without a thought, but Dane caught her hand firmly and looked at the other two men.

"What do you think?" he asked softly.

They had approached the mine obliquely, and now stood a few yards away behind the cover of a riotous clump of bushes.

Eyeing a trickle of water that escaped a narrow ventilation shaft low on the side of the hill and had worn a deep trench, Kelsey said with a sigh, "All I think is that if we go in there, we're going to get our feet wet."

"They went in," Derek observed. "You can see prints near the entrance. Any idea how deep the shaft is?" he asked Dane.

"No, but it was worked for years. My guess is that there are dozens of separate tunnels, at least half of them flooded."

After a moment Derek said, "I noticed something back in the house. There was a big hurricane lantern on the mantel in the living room, filled with kerosene. Most of these remote houses keep that kind of thing around in case the power goes."

"Makes sense," Dane said, and then, his eyes sharpening, added, "There should have been two of them?"

Derek nodded. "I checked, because the mantel looked unbalanced. The place was a bit dusty, but there was a clear circle at the other end of the mantel, and it matched the base of the lamp."

Kelsey was staring toward the mine. "So whichever of them has the lamp has the edge . . . or just may present a nice, clear target."

"We have to go in," Katrina said impatiently.

"Easy," Dane said to soothe her. "We will. But we have to be careful how we do it. Skye might still be looking for Adrian somewhere in one of those tunnels."

"He might be hurt." She choked.

"He isn't." Dane's voice was calm and certain. "Not yet, anyway."

Kelsey eyed him. "It's like that with you two?"

"Yes. A blessing at the moment, but remind me to tell you about the time Skye dropped everything and flew two thousand miles to get home because I'd broken a finger." Before anyone could comment, he said, "We'll have to stay together and take care with the light. Once we're in there, we may hear something. We don't even know if Adrian's aware he's been followed, so we can't make any noise to alert him."

They moved forward cautiously, slipping around the splintering timbers bracing the opening and remaining close to the wall. They went a good twenty feet into the tunnel before Kelsey turned on the flashlight and narrowed the beam with his fingers, directing it downward so that it provided only enough faint light to prevent them from tripping over fallen timbers and rubble.

And the dark, musty earth swallowed them.

Katrina was only vaguely aware that Dane still held her hand firmly, and she didn't think much about the darkness or close walls. She didn't feel smothered or panicked. She wouldn't realize until much later that the most powerful and paralyzing fear of her life was gone, driven out forever by a greater fear.

All her senses were reaching, probing the darkness in an intense, desperate need. She could hear only the hollow, incessant dripping of water; she was aware of the clammy, chilly sensation of damp; and the dark, musky smell of the buried earth filled her nose. Like the others except for Derek, who was apparently unarmed, she held her gun ready.

They found the first branching in the shaft about fifty feet inside, but their silent exploration ended quickly when the tunnel led into a pool of black water. They retraced their steps and went on. The second offshoot curved gently for thirty feet and ended back in the main shaft. A third and fourth tunnel were each blocked, one by a cave-in and the other by water.

The footing beneath them was increasingly damp, but it was obvious that the water that had once flooded the main shaft had washed away the rubble that littered the floor closer to the entrance. They had less worry of falling over something, but it became more and more difficult to walk without slipping, and the walls sweated.

An occasional creaking groan shattered the quiet from time to time as the earth settled on the shoulders of ancient timbers. The hollow *plunk* of dripping water was louder now, and they gradually became conscious of a rushing sound, almost beneath the level of awareness at first. It was like the sound heard when one holds a big seashell to the ear: the ghostly echoes of a phantom ocean trapped for eons.

Dane, who was leading the way, stopped suddenly and stiffened. Instinctively Katrina tried to penetrate the darkness and see his face, because she had heard nothing that might have alerted him and she was terrified that he had felt something. His hand tightened around hers briefly, and then he was moving swiftly forward again, sacrificing caution for speed.

They hadn't gone a half dozen steps before the sharp reports of gunfire bounced off the walls. Almost as quickly, the sounds stopped with chilling abruptness.

Katrina caught the sound of a curse from Kelsey, no louder than a breath, and then Dane was slowing, moving cautiously once again. The mine shaft curved to the left, and as they went another few feet they could see a dim glow ahead of them; it brightened slightly until Kelsey could turn off the flashlight he carried. Dane slowed even more, moving with absolute silence. Then he stopped.

The others all eased toward him, peering around him to see what had stopped him.

It was a cavern fully fifty feet across and possibly more; the light from a hurricane lantern perched precariously on a boulder reached only that far. This was without a doubt the source of the mine's failure. It was obvious that water had been in this place a long time, and it still moved sluggishly with whispering sounds, perhaps still fed by an underground river.

There were a number of boulders, possibly freed by the explosion that had ripped an opening into the cavern, and the water level had receded at least thirty feet from the doorway. Between the doorway and the water the floor glistened wetly, and it was clear to each of the four that is was very slippery.

The two men struggling twenty feet away could hardly keep to their feet.

Katrina wanted to race forward, to do something, *anything* except stand there with her heart in her throat and fear for Skye clawing her mind. But Dane's whisper, inaudible from a foot away, held her motionless.

"Are you a good enough shot?" he asked her. "I'm not." He looked at Kelsey, who instantly shook his head even though the big automatic in his hand was leveled and ready; he wasn't willing to try it either, as long as he had a choice.

In the flickering light of the lamp they could see the violence of the struggle, both men twisting and striving to overpower the other. There was no clear target, no chance of getting Adrian without hitting Skye as well. And Katrina knew why they couldn't just rush in to help Skye. His face was taut with utter concentration, and if he were distracted by anything at all, it was likely that Adrian would be able to stab him with the long, wicked knife that was poised just inches from Skye's chest.

Neither man was making a sound, and their total silence was more horrifying than any curses they could have voiced. It was a grim, deadly struggle, a battle of sheer brute strength, and it was obvious that the two were evenly matched.

The knife had blood on it. Katrina saw the blood, and she choked back a cry of pain and fear when she saw more blood on Skye. He had taken off his jacket at some point, and she could see that somewhere beneath his concealing black T-shirt he was wounded, because there was blood on his left arm, too much blood.

And that, she realized numbly, was why the big men were evenly matched. Skye had lost a great deal of blood, somehow Adrian had wounded him, and his strength was draining away, his luck deserting him. Adrian, uninjured and as icily soulless as Skye was fierily alive, focused all his madman's strength in the implacable intention of destroying his enemy.

But Skye's luck hadn't entirely deserted him. Adrian, trying to brace his feet to get more leverage for his straining arms, was just unbalanced enough so that when his shoe came down on an especially slippery place he began falling. And Skye instantly fell, with him, landing on him hard.

With the knife between them.

That was when Dane released Katrina's hand and ran forward into the cavern. All of them ran because the two men had fallen behind a boulder, and they couldn't see what had happened. . . .

Skye didn't feel any pain. He had at first, when the knife had gone into him, a hot agony that had taken his breath. But then the struggle with Adrian had demanded all his concentration, and he hadn't had time to feel the pain. Some distant, detached part of his mind had warned that he was losing blood fast, and the easy strength that had never been a conscious thing had gradually required his fierce will to hold steady. His muscles had quivered and the breath had rasped in his throat, and exhaustion had battered at him as relentlessly as his enemy did.

Furious at the ebbing of his strength, he had fought the black wave threatening to wash over him and forced his trembling muscles to offer their last ounce of power. And then he had felt himself falling, and he thought he had wrenched the knife aside at the last moment, but he wasn't sure because everything was so utterly dark and silent.

He was very tired, and not much interested in doing anything about the darkness. He would have let it carry him peacefully away, except that something tugged at him, resisting. And, gradually, he felt a surge of impatience at the darkness. It hid things from him, and he didn't like things hidden.

He felt the tug again, and obeyed it this time, ignoring the seductive darkness as he began fighting his way toward the light. He was aware of movement first, and the sensation of coldness, and he heard an annoying roar that was too loud because someone was saying something to him and he couldn't hear it.

But he was warmer now, and the darkness was less intense, and whatever had pulled him this far was holding on tight. There was something familiar about that, and he considered the matter idly. It was . . . a connection . . . to someone. A link. That was it. But it wasn't the link he remembered, it was a new connection, a different and stronger one, and he thought he wasn't accustomed to it yet. It was disturbing, but he had the notion that it was something he had wanted terribly.

He didn't feel alone anymore.

He was aware of a deep surge of satisfaction. He'd gotten it, finally. He wasn't entirely sure what it meant, except it made him happier than he could ever remember being. There was someone he was connected to, someone who couldn't hide from him anymore.

Eight

Skye was lucky, but he was also human. He had been injured before in the line of duty. Given his recklessness, if he had escaped injury in ten years it wouldn't have been remarkable, it would have been a miracle. But Dane hadn't been wrong in saying his brother believed he was made of iron. It wasn't a conscious thing, but like all men gifted with extraordinary luck, Skye was always surprised when it deserted him. And he was shocked, on some deep level of himself, to find himself vulnerable.

So when he fought his way to consciousness with only a vague memory of what had happened, his first and strongest emotion was sheer annoyance. "Damn," he muttered hoarsely, forcing his eyes to open. Matching eyes were looking down at him, and an almost-matching face wearing a mustache looked grimly amused by the curse.

"Don't try to move," Dane warned, then sighed as Skye of course did and bit back a groan. "In case you've forgotten, Adrian stuck a knife into you. You lost a hell of a lot of blood. Now, for God's sake, *be still.*"

Skye closed his eyes until the wave of sick dizziness passed. He felt appallingly weak, and the pain in the region of his left shoulder throbbed as if someone were still stabbing him, again and again. He thought he'd been almost conscious a few times before this, but he wasn't sure; his fuzzy mind held only the dim recollection of voices and touches and pain. In any case, he was fully awake now. And the pain was a constant thing. After a few moments he opened his eyes cautiously and ignored the pain. He was in bed, he realized. In Katrina's bed. "Where's Trina?" he asked his brother.

Dane nodded toward the closed door leading to the den. "Talking to the doctor. I told her you were too mean to die on her, and once the doctor confirmed the truth of what I said, I think she made up her mind to kill you herself."

Skye frowned, trying to make sense of that. Katrina had been angry, he remembered, but that had happened long before he'd left the park, and he had been certain he'd managed to win her forgiveness. "She's mad at me?"

Leaning back in the armchair that had been placed by the bed, Dane surveyed his twin with rueful amusement. "I suppose it never occurred to you that she would be?"

"No." Skye was baffled. "I knew she was a little upset, but she didn't seem to be mad when I left."

"My mistake, I suppose," Dane said.

After staring at him for a moment, Skye said, "How did I get back here? Adrian—"

"Is back at the house, with Daniel and a couple of his marshals standing guard. He has a concussion because he hit his head on a rock when you both went down. And you got back here through no doing of your own."

Despite the curve of firm lips that most people would have taken to be a smile, Skye wasn't deceived. Taking note of and correctly reading the steely light in the eyes so like his own, he prudently remained silent while he hastily considered his options. He had seen Dane truly enraged so rarely that he could have counted the occasions on the fingers of one hand even after thirty-five years; but massive earthquakes, Skye had decided, seldom rocked the same section of real estate more than once in a century.

Dane's temper was like an earthquake, and though Skye was all too apt to wave red flags at bulls of all varieties, he tended to avoid angering his brother. This time, however, it was obvious that he had outdone himself.

"I'm a wounded man," Skye offered, eyeing Dane warily.

"I realize that." Dane's voice was deceptively polite. "I could hardly help but realize it, since hauling your carcass out of that mine shaft is destined to be one of my more enduring memories."

Skye winced. "Sorry," he said, and there was real remorse in his voice. He could imagine what Dane had gone through.

Dane wasn't quite ready to forgive. "Between trying to stop you bleeding to death and at the same time to get you out of that hole in the ground as quickly as possible, Katrina, Derek, and I had our hands full. Kelsey just slung Adrian over one shoulder since he was out cold, but we had to be a bit more careful with you."

"Katrina?" Skye stared at him, forcing his sluggish mind to begin working again. "She was there? Wait a minute. This doesn't make sense."

"You're telling me."

Oddly enough, Skye had never lost his own temper with his brother, and didn't now. "Dane, what happened?"

After a moment Dane said, "Katrina came straight to me after you'd left. I was out in the park, with Derek and Kelsey. We decided to take the helicopter Josh had standing by in case it was needed. Katrina said she was coming with us, and I had better sense than to argue with her. When we got to the house, we found the map, and I remembered the mine. After that it was just a matter of getting there and inside, and trying to find you. We were close when we heard the gunfire, but by the time we reached the cavern, it was impossible to get a shot at Adrian without hitting you as well. We had to wait."

Skye was staring at the ceiling, his eyes holding a strange, vibrant light. Absently he said, "The bastard must have known someone was following him, though I'll swear I never made a sound to alert him. He'd hidden in the cavern with his lamp on a boulder and the flame turned down low. When I came in, he threw a knife at me. Got me, too, damn him. While I was pulling the knife out, he turned up the lamp and started shooting."

Dane was watching him intently. "The shots didn't last long," he noted.

"No." Skye's lips twisted. "It would have been funny if he hadn't been trying to kill me. We both slipped. Can you beat that? Professionals sliding like clowns in the mud, and our guns going flying. The guns landed in the water, where I'd thrown the knife. I didn't find out Adrian had a second knife until he charged me with it. I think he got me a couple more times, but not seriously."

"That first time did the damage," Dane told him. "Nicked an artery. That's why you were losing blood so fast."

Skye nodded, then grimaced as the motion sent a jolt of pain through his body. "There seemed to be a lot of it, but I didn't have time to try to stop it. I don't remember much more before I blacked out, except that I was trying to get that damned knife away from him. Did I?"

"More or less. You managed not to stab yourself with it when you fell on him. You cracked three of his ribs, by the way."

"I think he cracked a couple of mine," Skye noted, suddenly conscious of a constriction lower than the heavy bandages on his left shoulder and upper chest.

"He did." Dane sighed. "Once we got you back to the helicopter, we came straight back here. The closest doctor was the one Josh had stashed here just in case. We alerted Josh by radio, and the doctor was waiting for us. He pumped a few pints of blood into you—"

"Not all from you," Skye objected.

"No. Luckily for you, Derek, Rafferty, and Josh have the same blood type, and they volunteered. Anyway, the doc patched you up and strapped your ribs. He says you can't get up for a week." Smiling a little, Dane watched that sink in. "So let it be a lesson to you," he added dryly.

Skye was frowning. "I'll be up by tomorrow."

"No, you won't," said Katrina calmly from the doorway.

Turning his head cautiously to look at her, Skye's eyes lit again with that strange, vivid gleam. "Tomorrow," he repeated in a silky tone.

She was a little pale, but her lovely face was composed and her amber eyes were gazing steadily at him. "If you try to get up before next Friday," she said in a gentle voice with all the flexibility of tempered steel, "I'll shoot you myself."

Dane turned a sudden laugh into a cough.

Before Skye could respond to her threat, she added, "Dr. Randall says you can have some soup if you want. Are you hungry?"

"Yes. But not soup." Skye's eyes were veiled, but through the long lashes they looked brighter than ever.

She ignored that. "I'll call room service." Stepping back out into the den, she pulled the door shut again.

Dane watched his brother curiously, taking note of the long fingers, moving restlessly on the covers. Even his left hand was fidgety, and he shouldn't have been able to move it at all; that arm was in a sling to keep the shoulder immobile.

After a moment Dane said quietly, "She's been with you the whole time. More than twenty-four hours." He didn't add that Katrina, hollow-eyed and fierce, had refused all help but the doctor's in taking care of Skye.

Skye looked at him, a muscle in his jaw tightening. "You said she—went into that mine?"

"I didn't try to stop her," Dane admitted. "Couldn't have. She was hell-bent on going in after you."

A rough breath escaped Skye. "Dane, ever since she was a child, Trina's been claustrophobic."

Dane returned that intense gaze, then smiled a little. "I don't think she even noticed." He rose to his feet, and changed the subject. "Do you want to eat lying flat on your back, or would you like to try sitting up a bit?"

The process of being raised and propped up against several pillows brought a film of sweat to Skye's pale face, but with Dane's deft help it wasn't as painful as it might have been. "Thanks," he muttered, and lifted his right hand to his face experimentally; it shook a bit, and his arm felt leaden, but at least he could move. "I need a shave," he realized.

"You look like hell," his twin told him frankly.

The comment reassured Skye somewhat, because he hadn't been sure if his brother was still furious with him. He had no doubt that Dane would swear at him later, but for now he seemed to have calmed down about the situation.

Breathing carefully to avoid jarring his cracked ribs, Skye said. "What about Hagen?"

"No problem." Dane touched one finger to the neat mustache adorning his upper lip. "I'll get rid of this and borrow some of your clothes; he won't know the difference. There's nothing much doing until Saturday anyway. Josh was here earlier, and I told him there was no reason to cancel the caper."

"Of course there isn't," Skye said. "And I'll be back on my feet in a day or two."

Dane shook his head slightly, but said, "I'll go and tell the others you're firmly back among the living."

"It was that close?" Skye was startled.

"Too close." Dane's voice was grim.

Skye said roughly, "I'm sorry."

Dane knew Skye wasn't sorry for having risked his life. Given the same situation, Skye would act exactly the same way again. He was sorry only that others had been worried. He couldn't know, Dane thought, that they'd been scared half to death. Sighing, Dane said, "One of these days . . ."

Skye smiled suddenly, the crooked smile that was as rare and unexpected as it was disarming. "Yeah, I know."

Dane went to the door and opened it, stepping back to allow Katrina to carry in a tray. Addressing her, he said, "If you need any help keeping that renegade where he's supposed to be, let me know. I'll come and sit on him."

"Don't worry," she replied serenely.

Skye looked at her a bit uncertainly as his chuckling brother left and Katrina approached the bed. He had searched her face eagerly the moment he had first seen her, but although what Dane had told him seemed to indicate that she felt a great deal more for him than just desire, he hadn't been able to find any evidence of it in her calm expression or steady eyes.

She wasn't hiding from him exactly, and she wasn't aloof, but he had never seen her so utterly tranquil. Her very calm was like a barrier, rock-steady. And he'd never seen her eyes so dark and still. It puzzled him and made him uneasy, and he could feel his heart clench inside his chest as he wondered if she had somehow put herself totally beyond his reach. He wanted to ask but was afraid to.

Katrina leaned over to set the bed tray across his lap, then straightened. "I don't suppose you'll let me feed you," she said somewhat dryly.

"Of course not." He stared at the tray, and worry made him irritable. "I hate soup."

"Too bad," she said, sitting down in the chair by the bed. "The doctor says you eat soup, then you eat soup."

She met his brooding look steadily, and after a moment he picked up a spoon with his right hand and began eating. Hardly conscious of her own exhaustion, Katrina sat quietly in the chair and watched him, resisting the urge to reach over and push the tumbled black hair off his brow. He was pale and clearly annoyed by his physical weakness, and she thought he was probably disgusted by the injuries that reminded him he was vulnerable.

She wouldn't soon forget her own terror at that reminder. Even though she had know he could be hurt, there had been some part of her that had trusted in his amazing inner fire. But he had lain in this bed, utterly still for the first time in her memory, and the vibrant life force inside him had dwindled to only a flickering spark. His skin had been cool to her touch; those incredible eyes closed against her. . . .

Not all the reassurances of Dane or the doctor had convinced her that he wouldn't die, not during those first long hours when she had sat, her eyes fixed on his face, everything inside her willing him not to leave her. Then, gradually, she had seen the change in him, as if the indomitable spirit he held with such careless indifference within him had begun rebuilding the fire. His pulse had steadied and strengthened, and his skin had warmed slowly.

The doctor had suspected a fever at first, and had been surprised. "Odd," he'd said to Katrina. "His temperature's normal, but his skin—"

"That's normal too," Katrina had murmured, so weak with relief she had felt faint. "For him."

"Must have a high metabolic rate," Dr. Randall had muttered to himself.

After that she had believed Skye would make it. In a natural reaction she had been fiercely angry then that he had dared to risk getting killed. Dane had been sympathetic, listening silently and with twitching lips to her muttered and somewhat incoherent threats against his currently defenseless twin. He had suggested that she take a relaxing shower, since there was no longer a need for someone to be constantly with Skye, and her sudden realization of the dried blood on her clothes had sent her scurrying to the bathroom.

Now, more than twenty-four hours after Skye's injury, Katrina was in a strange state of tranquility. She felt limp, almost numb, and curiously peaceful.

She looked at him as he reluctantly finished the hated soup, and she felt a wave of love wash over her with such force that she could only endure it silently.

He was complex and temperamental, sometimes thoughtless and often graceless, and he had a terrifying habit of risking his neck without hesitation. Becoming a part of his life would be like sailing off toward the ends of the earth to find out if dragons lived there: a dangerous, potentially heartbreaking and altogether spectacular adventure.

Katrina wasn't worried. She could swim. Whether he liked it or not, she intended to sail off with him. He might well feel nothing but desire for her—but he did feel that. It was something to build on, and she wasn't afraid anymore.

"Don't look at me like that," he said suddenly.

She looked at the soup bowl instead and, seeing that he had finished, got up to take the tray back into the den. He caught her wrists as she leaned over the bed, his hand warm and hard.

"I didn't mean that," he said in a voice that was low and rapid. "I want you to look at me. But you've never looked at me like that before, and I don't know what it means." He released her wrist as she grasped the tray and straightened.

Katrina looked down at him for a moment, loving him so much she could hardly bear it. Softly she said, "It means I hope you haven't gotten rid of that demon yet."

He frowned and, in a totally blank voice, said, "Demon?"

She turned away from the bed and carried the tray back into the den. He shouted her name twice before she could return, and she came back into the bedroom to find him grimacing, his right hand clamped to his left shoulder. He had probably tried to get up, she realized, and before she could say anything about his stubbornness, he was holding that unrestrained hand out commandingly.

"Come here," he ordered, his eyes fierce.

Katrina came to the bed and sank down carefully on the edge as he caught her wrist and tugged. "You'll start to bleed again if you keep moving," she said worriedly.

He shook his head impatiently. "What the hell is all this about demons?" he demanded.

She couldn't help but smile, realizing that he had no memory of what he's said to her. Entirely typical, of course, that he didn't remember harsh words. Fighting a surge of hope, she said, "It's what you said that first day. That what you—what you felt for me was like a demon you couldn't get rid of. I just hope you haven't gotten rid of it, that's all."

He was still frowning, but his gaze held that hard, searching look. "Why?" he asked tersely.

Katrina drew a breath and answered, "Because I love you." The sudden blazing ferocity in his eyes shook her, and she added unsteadily, "I know you can't love me, but I'll stay with you as long as you want me—"

The hand holding her wrist yanked her abruptly down to him and his arm was like iron around her. "I love you so much I'm insane with it." he growled, locking his fingers in her hair to hold her firmly while he kissed her.

She had her hands braced on either side of him, aware, even in her bursting happiness, of his injuries and trying not to give in to the insistent pressure of his arm. It was hard to think at all, and even harder to speak when he finally let her draw back just a little.

"Skye, your ribs . . . your shoulder . . ."

He wasn't listening. There was an expression on his lean, beautiful face she'd never seen before, and the light in his eyes was so bright it was like sunshine. "I thought I was going to lose you again," he said thickly. "You kept hiding from me, and I was going crazy trying to hold on to you."

She lifted one hand and touched his cheek, her heart catching when he turned his head to press his lips into her palm. "I—I thought it was just passion," she whispered.

"You were the only one. Even Hagen knew the instant he saw me looking at you. Lord, Trina, I never stopped loving you. When I found you here, the only thing I could think of was to make sure I wouldn't lose you again. I knew I could make you want me, and it seemed like the only hope I had."

"I was afraid," she confessed simply. "You—there's so much intensity in you, so much force. And after that first day, I was convinced you were just trying to—to get rid of that demon."

"I couldn't have said that," he protested.

"You did."

He was smiling. "Maybe. Heaven knows I don't know what I'm saying half the time around you. I knew I was pushing, but I couldn't stop myself."

"I noticed," she said.

His smiled took on a sensual heat and his hand slipped under the tail of her shirt to find the smooth skin of her back. "Can I help it if I can't keep my hands off you?"

"Apparently not." She kept her face straight with an effort, catching his hand and removing it firmly. "You should rest. It's after midnight, and—"

"I don't want to rest."

Fighting to ignore the hungry glitter in his eyes, she said, "I won't let you delay your recovery just because—"

"Tell me you love me," he ordered.

Feeling herself weaken, she evaded his reaching hand and stood up. "I love you, Skye!" Hastily she bent to prevent him from flinging back the covers. "Dammit, you're going to start bleeding again!"

"So what?" He was working his left arm out of the sling, ignoring the protest of his shoulder. "Just let me get rid of this damned thing—"

"No!" She caught both his hands tightly. "Skye, be reasonable. You've been hurt."

"Nothing important was hurt," he drawled.

Katrina couldn't help but glance at his lower body, feeling heat rush through her at the clear evidence of his arousal, but she managed a glare at him when he chuckled.

"Climb in here with me," he invited.

"I'll sleep on the couch."

An implacable determination flashed in his eyes. Softly he said, "Try that, sweetheart, and I'll be on the couch with you. From now on you aren't sleeping anywhere except with me."

Wryly aware that Dane had been right when he'd said she might have to practice a bit before being able to stop Skye once he'd set his mind on doing something reckless, she sighed and tried a compromise. "If I stay here, will you promise to rest? If you don't, I swear I'll call Dr. Randall and have him give you a shot."

"Him and what army?"

Katrina glared at him and waited.

Finally Skye said, "Hell. All right. I promise."

Then minutes later, after prudently undressing in the bathroom and changing into an overlarge, button-up sleep shirt that was gaily striped in yellow and wasn't very sexy, Katrina bent over Skye to remove the pillows propping him up and ease him back flat again.

Her shirt gaped away from her breasts as she bent over him, and Skye half closed his eyes and groaned softly. "Let me take back the promise." His right hand was already reaching for her when she straightened abruptly.

She stared down at him. "What am I going to do with you?"

He was quite willing to tell her, but he had a feeling she'd sleep on the couch if he did. And, stubborn words aside, he knew damned well he'd fall flat on his face if he tried to get out of the bed. He also knew that he couldn't make love to her yet, no matter how badly he wanted to and no matter how much the throbbing fullness of his loins insisted.

He decided he'd better heal fast.

"Just let me hold you," he said finally.

Her eyes softened with that warm, steady glow that had baffled him earlier. She turned off the lamp on the nightstand on his side of the bed, then went around and cautiously slipped beneath the covers on his right. The moment she turned off the lamp on that nightstand, he reached out and pulled her firmly against his side.

"I don't want to hurt you," she whispered.

Skye cradled her close, drawing her head down to rest on his uninjured shoulder and smoothing her wild, silky curls. "You aren't," he told her gently, ignoring the pain. He had never felt any pain so strong that it would have kept him from holding her, and he doubted he ever would.

Within minutes she was asleep, curled up beside him boneless as a cat. She was exhausted, he knew, worn out from watching over him all those hours. Skye held her close and stared into the darkness for a long time, remembering how everything inside him had splintered when she had told him she loved im. He still felt that way, shaken and stunned, ardly daring to believe that he wouldn't lose her gain.

For six years she had never been out of his mind, nd no matter how may times he had told himself avagely to forget her, just a glimpse of wild, curling ed hair had had the power to stop his heart. He adn't told her, but he had returned to Germany hree times during the last years, ignoring Daniel tuart's warnings that it could be dangerous. He ad gone back and searched for her, returning al-ays to the apartment where someone else lived and earing himself to pieces because he couldn't find er.

His arm tightened around her as he remembered hat pain, but the last echoes faded away as she numbled in her sleep and cuddled close.

He had found her now, and he'd never let her go.

Skye woke early in the morning, feeling much tronger than he had the night before. Katrina was till deeply asleep, missing the dawn for the first ime since they'd been together again. He shifted xperimentally and winced when both his shoulder nd his ribs protested. But he was determined that atrina wouldn't have to wait on him hand and foot or the next few days and, besides, there were some hings a man preferred to do for himself.

So he clamped his teeth together hard and care-ully moved his arm from around Katrina so he could it up. His head swam dizzily for a few moments, nd his ribs gave him merry hell, especially when he wung his legs off the bed. He felt her stir behind im, but then she sighed and went still again.

When the room stopped spinning, he used his

good arm to lever himself up and onto his feet. An
if he hadn't taken a hasty step and grabbed the bac
of the high-backed visitor's chair, he would ha
fallen flat on his face. Damn! He was as weak as
sick cat, and every muscle was so sore, it felt as
someone had been beating him with a stick. A co
sweat popped out all over him, and he had to u
the support of the chair for long minutes with h
eyes closed.

He was finally able to move, then worked his wa
cautiously along the wall to the bathroom door. Ma
ing it, he eased inside and pushed the door soft
closed. There were plenty of things to hold on to
there, and he was grateful. But he had a hell of
time shaving because he needed his good hand ar
couldn't use the other to brace himself.

Idly he decided that Katrina was going to be ma
as hell. But that was all right. Now that he knew sh
loved him, he wouldn't mind when she got mad
him. And she was bound to from time to time. F
thought there would probably be some glorious figh
between them because he had a thoughtless temp
and that red hair of hers wasn't at all as deceptive a
he'd once believed.

She was just stirring awake as he braced himse
in the doorway of the bathroom, and her lovely ey
blinked at him sleepily when she sat up. Then, su
denly, she was fully awake. Amber fire lit her eye
and she flung back the covers.

Her sleep shirt had ridden up to the tops of h
thighs, and he felt his weakened body harden wit
an instant surge of desire. A primal sound he wa
unaware of making rumbled up from the depths
his chest as she reached him, and he forgot to brac
himself because his good hand was sliding dow
her side to shape firm, rounded flesh.

"What are you doing?" she gasped, slipping her shoulder under his good arm for support.

"Lord, you feel good," he muttered.

Muttering herself, Katrina removed his hand from her bottom and placed it firmly on her shoulder. "You have to get back into bed," she told him, her arms around him as she tried to brace him without hurting him.

Skye knew he'd been on his feet too long, and cursed his trembling muscles as he let her help him. He told himself he still lacked the strength to be a lover, but the reminder did nothing to reduce his aching need for her. He loved her, and he wanted to hear her say she loved him while she was writhing in his arms, while passion exploded in them both. . . .

"You shaved!" she accused him.

The prosaic exclamation drove the heated images from his mind, and Skye settled back onto his pillows with the ghost of a laugh. Looking at her as she bent to pull the covers over him, he couldn't resist saying, "I said I'd be on my feet today."

"And I said I'd shoot you!" she snapped.

He didn't mind her temper, but he didn't like her to be worried about him. "Sweetheart, I know what I'm doing. If I stayed here for a week, I'd be useless for another one. I've been through this before, and—" He broke off, sorry that he'd said that.

She sank down on the edge of the bed, staring at him. Her bottom lip quivered suddenly. "You don't have any scars," she whispered.

He took her hand and carried it to his lips briefly. "No. I don't scar. In a few months you won't be able to find any sign of this wound either." Trying to get her mind off past injuries, he went on. "I won't do too much, I promise. I'll get plenty of rest. But I have to get up and move around some."

Katrina could feel her resolve weakening. Half angrily she said, "I'm going to call Dr. Randall and see what he says."

"Fine," Skye returned promptly.

She was a little suspicious of his quick agreement, but when the doctor examined Skye a couple of hours later, he confirmed what Skye had said.

"Well, you're healing faster than I expected," he told Skye dryly. "If you feel well enough to be up and about, go ahead. Just take it slow."

Katrina stared at him reproachfully, and Skye held one hand over his bound ribs while he laughed at her.

Later in the day Dane told her that he'd expected it. "Once he's conscious," he told her, "Skye heals fast. And he'd too impatient to stay in bed. If he broke every bone in his body and they put him in a cast head to toe, he'd probably wear roller skates to get around."

Skye, who was sitting on the couch in the den wearing only a pair of sweat pants, grinned at her. Katrina mentally threw up her hands in surrender, but irritably told Dane, "You're a lot of help!"

"Sorry." He smiled at her. Without his mustache, and dressed in the casual dark clothing Skye usually wore, he was the image of his brother. He had even imperceptibly altered his way of moving, and his normally lazy drawl held the more clipped and rapid cadence of Skye's speech.

Katrina had observed those last traits when she had earlier gone to give Gigi a progress report on Skye. Dane had been there with Hagen, and Katrina had made a plausible excuse to draw her friend out of the office. She couldn't have very well told Gigi about Skye's recovery when Hagen had believed the man to be standing right beside him.

"You'll probably be having other visitors today,"

Dane told his brother now, not without a certain enjoyment. "Everybody wants to come and swear at you. I told them you were up to it."

"Thanks," Skye said dryly.

Others did come, all of them at some time or other during the day. And if they didn't swear at Skye, they nonetheless made it clear that the next time he was involved in a team effort and decided to play the Lone Ranger, there would be an abundance of people standing in line to express their displeasure.

Meekness was hardly one of Skye's character traits, but by the end of the day he was a bit subdued. Not because of what he'd done, of course, but by the reactions to it. He had never been much of a team player; his professional partnership with Dane stretched back over ten years, but that was far more a blood bond than one of collaboration. He was unaccustomed to people worrying about him, and more than a little surprised by it.

"I hope you aren't going to yell at me," he told Katrina with some feeling that night.

"They didn't yell." She was standing by the dresser brushing her hair, and sent him an amused look over her shoulder. "But whether you like it or not, they care about you. All of them. And they were right."

Skye had spent the day very determinedly gaining strength, and as he watched her now he felt familiar stirrings. He forgot about people yelling at him. "Trina," he said.

She looked at him again, this time with instant awareness and a certain amount of helplessness. Her knees felt weak all of a sudden, and she was hardly aware of putting the brush down and turning toward the bed. "You need to rest," she protested.

"I need you," he said, and the stark truth of that made his voice ragged.

Katrina came to the bed slowly, her heart pounding. She felt hot and weak, and already conscious of the throbbing emptiness only he could fill. Skye threw the covers back as she reached him, then pulled her down on the bed beside him.

She gasped. "Your ribs."

"To hell with my ribs." He was unbuttoning her sleep shirt with the fingers of one hand, but it wasn't quick enough for him, and he pulled his left arm from the sling so he could use that hand as well. Katrina moaned a wordless protest, but when she met his eyes and saw the fiery hunger there, she stopped trying to make him remember his injuries. That look told her plainly that he didn't give a damn whether he hurt himself, because he wanted her right that minute and he wasn't going to wait. She had seen enough of his relentless will by now to know when to stop fighting it.

She helped him get rid of the sleep shirt, and when his hot, hard hands surrounded her breasts, she almost cried out with pleasure. Her body was so attuned to him, so responsive to his urgency, she was instantly out of control. But some final shred of reason made her try to keep him from moving any more than necessary. And it was a new pleasure to love him as he had so often loved her, to touch and kiss his powerful body with a hunger of her own until he groaned and shuddered.

Skye endured the sweet torment of her touch for as long as he could, but his control quickly shattered, and he lifted her bodily above him, a half-wild cry tearing from his throat. She settled over him with a lithe grace, her cat's eyes gleaming down at him, and when her tight heat surrounded him, he thought he'd go out of his mind with the searing pleasure of it.

"Tell me," he ordered in a voice that was almost gone, his hard hands on her hips guiding her slow movements.

"I love you," she said huskily, staring into his narrowed, fiercely intent eyes. The tension coiling inside her was an agony of suspension, and she almost moaned out the words again and again, whimpering when he quickened the pace and surged beneath her with no awareness of his injuries or any consciousness of pain except the pain of hot desire.

And, as always, there was no slow ascent for either of them, but rather a swift, relentless, shattering climb that hurled them wildly over the brink. She collapsed on his chest with a wordless cry, feeling him shudder and hold her hard as a guttural groan was wrenched from him.

Katrina couldn't move for a long time; even the awareness of his bandages beneath her cheek and a niggling worry about his injuries lacked the power to make her move.

"I love you, Trina," he said.

She lifted her head and looked at him, and the love glowing in his eyes nearly stopped her heart. "I love you too," she whispered, shifting just far enough so she could kiss him. Then, worried, she said, "Your ribs—"

Arms tightening around her, Skye said, "To hell with my ribs."

Nine

Raven opened the door to let Dane into the suite, then led the way into the sitting room where Josh was just hanging up the phone. Looking at their visitor, Josh said, "Everything set for tomorrow morning?"

Dane nodded and sat down in a chair while Raven joined her husband on the couch. "No problems, far as I can see. The governor's due to arrive just after the park opens, so the crowd won't be too large. Since all of you *and* the other people you've planted around the park will be near the Ferris wheel, we shouldn't attract much more than mild interest."

Josh nodded slightly. "Everyone's been briefed. They'll have a cover story if any visitors have questions."

Lifting one eyebrow, Dane said, "A cover story?"

"We're making a movie," Raven interjected. She nodded toward a video camera lying nearby on a table. "Just some preliminary shots, you understand."

Dane grinned. "Neat."

She smiled in return, then said, "How's Skye? I

dropped by Katrina's suite a couple of days ago but didn't stay long. I got the feeling they wanted to be alone."

Chuckling, Dane said. "Skye's fine. He could have gone back to being himself three days ago, but when I told him to stay put, he didn't argue. Gigi says she'll have to find another manager for her hotel."

"Speaking of Gigi," Raven said, "how's she doing?"

Dane eyed her. "Don't you mean how's your *other* little plot progressing?" he asked gently.

Josh smiled, but Raven looked innocent. "Plot? Why, I don't know what you mean."

Dane made a rude sound.

Raven didn't lose her innocent expression, but her eyes gleamed merrily. Blandly she said, "Can I help it if Gigi's a very attractive woman? And if Daniel Stuart's a very handsome man?"

Dane had to laugh. "No, and don't try to tell me that both of them aren't in on it. Daniel's just having too much fun, and Gigi's almost purring."

"What about Hagen?" Josh asked, grinning.

"Steamed," Dane answered. "First Daniel got the directorship Hagen had earmarked for himself, and now he's after Gigi. She's playing it perfectly, a lot of dignity but definite interest; and Daniel's showing all the signs of losing his heart. Hagen can hardly stand to be in the same room with Daniel, and he's started watching over Gigi like a hawk."

Raven pursed her lips thoughtfully. "Is the maestro just mad, or is he worried?"

Dane looked thoughtful, his eyes abstracted as he watched Josh light a cigarette. Slowly he answered, "I'd say that at first it was sheer rage. But when Gigi started to—uh—encourage Daniel, it shook Hagen up. He hasn't had his mind on business the last couple of days." Clearing his throat, Dane added, "I happened to remark to him this morning that catching an assassin would certainly make Daniel mad, since he's been after Adrian as long as Hagen has. He perked right up."

Raven giggled. "And you say *I'm* devious."

"Well, I thought it'd be a shame if the final act of this little caper fell apart because Hagen had lost interest."

"Nice going," Josh told him.

"Thank you." Dane was polite.

"I wonder if he needs another push," Raven said thoughtfully.

Dane gazed at her for a moment, then said, "You're ruthless."

She widened her eyes at him. "Why? As Serena told me, you just arrange the circumstances to achieve a desired effect and point your players in the right direction. What happens is purely a matter of free will."

Josh chuckled as Dane gave him a faintly horrified look. "I know, it sounds scary as hell. But since I grew up with Serena, it doesn't shake me up anymore. I didn't know Raven had the talent when I married her, but I must admit she keeps me on my toes."

Raven looked at each of the men with pitying eyes. "I just decided that Hagen had been taking Gigi for granted, and she agreed with me. That's a very stupid thing to do, taking a woman for granted, even after twenty years."

"I'll keep that in mind," Josh murmured.

"So will I," Dane echoed, thinking of his Jenny, she of the Italian heritage and fiery temper.

Raven grinned at them. It was good to remind a man of these things, she reflected.

• • •

Hagen had had enough. His temper was uncertain at the best of times, though generally wielded with fine dramatic timing, and it was never more likely to explode than when his inner vision of himself as omniscient was challenged. He hated surprises when they were directed *at* him rather than orchestrated *by* him, and Gigi had surprised him.

He had never been quite certain of her—something he had admitted to himself only recently—but he had never expected her to look at another man with a purely personal interest in her fine eyes. And that it had to be Daniel. *Daniel!*

So when Hagen stormed into Gigi's suite without knocking late Friday afternoon, he was in the mood to pick a quarrel with an angel.

Nobody had ever accused Gigi of being an angel.

A book in hand, she had been relaxing in a corner of the long couch, but rose instantly to her feet, glaring at him. "How dare you!"

Hagen cast one thunderous look around the suite, and though he was relieved not to find Daniel there, it didn't show on his face. "I won't have it, Gigi!" he roared.

Gigi was a little woman, but there was nothing small about her temper. Drawing herself up to her full diminutive height, her eyes snapping, she said, "I have already told you, Hagen, *you do not command me.* My life is my own, and you have no right to interfere in it."

To his own astonishment, Hagen felt his towering rage descend with a lurch into shaken uncertainty. "But what are you doing?" he very nearly moaned. "And with *Daniel.* You've stabbed me in the back, and after all these years!"

She stared at him, unrelenting.

Hagen heard words tumbling out, and couldn't

believe they were coming from him. "You'd hate Washington, you know you would! And there's the park—your operation here—"

"I'm going to retire," she said calmly. "I have begun shutting down the operation already. I shall move into the country and raise racehorses."

He blinked. "What?"

Gigi kept her face straight with an effort. "Certainly. It will be amusing. And since I do not wish to live alone, I think I shall marry."

He blanched. "Not Daniel!"

"And why not? He is a handsome, distinguished man, and a complete gentleman. *He* would never take a woman for granted."

"Gigi—"

Inexorably she continued. "He is not arrogant, or manipulative, or egotistic, or deceitful. He respects my will, and would never try to make decisions for me. He would never rant and rave at me. He would not deviously try to arrange my life the moment my back is turned."

Hagen stared at her for a moment, and then his cupid's mouth curved suddenly in an unexpectedly humorous smile. "He'd bore you silly, my dear."

Her lips twitched responsively before she could stop them. Recovering, she snapped, "And he loves me!"

"But you love me," Hagen said.

With perfect calm she replied, "After twenty years I find that to love is not enough. I wish to *be* loved."

Hagen crossed the space between them with startling grace and speed for a man for his bulk, and there was a surprising strength in the arms that closed about her. "Dammit, you know I love you," he said almost irritably.

Gigi's slim form adapted itself easily to his girth,

but her lovely face remained unmoved. "I do not know that at all," she told him.

He glared at her. "I'm telling you. I love you. I've loved you for twenty years. Why would I keep coming around and dodging that damned sharp tongue of yours if I didn't love you?"

"Because nobody else stands up to you!" she retorted with spirit.

He chuckled suddenly. "True. You're a difficult woman, my dear, and in twenty years you've never bored me." He sighed, then said reflectively, "I suppose raising racehorses wouldn't be so bad. There's a certain challenge in that."

"I don't recall inviting you," she said sweetly.

Back on balance again, Hagen gave her an indulgent look. "Of course you did, Gigi. This little game you've been playing with Daniel was the invitation."

She eyed him ruefully. "Damn you."

He laughed again, but with rare grace admitted, "Well, it worked. Scared the hell out of me when I thought I was losing you. We'll get married as soon as possible."

As if addressing some third party, Gigi said, "I should have know he would tell rather than ask."

Hagen opened his eyes wide. "If you didn't mean to marry me, my dear, I'd like to know what kind of game you've been playing with me for twenty years."

Gigi might have sputtered at this unfair statement, but he didn't giver her the chance. Not that she minded.

Katrina had been a little worried that Skye might not trust in her love this time, but as the days passed it became obvious that whatever he had needed to make him certain he had found. The hard, searching look vanished from his eyes, and though he would never be a tranquil man, he was clearly less restless and far more at peace with himself.

Having once gained his feet, he healed with astonishing speed, and by the third day, Wednesday, had abandoned the elastic bandage over his ribs; he had also talked the doctor into reducing his other bandages, saying that this wounds would heal far more quickly if they weren't smothered by gauze.

Katrina, with glorious memories of his lovemaking in her mind, couldn't find the will to protest. Except for that first night, he hadn't made a single concession to his injuries. And since the admission of love between them had intensified an already overpowering desire, Katrina was all too aware that Skye's strength had returned full force.

Still, as she watched him shrugging easily into his shoulder harness early Saturday morning, she felt a pang of worry. It wasn't supposed to be dangerous, of course, but then, Adrian shouldn't have escaped either.

"Skye, I want to be there."

After pulling on a light Windbreaker, he came to her and pulled her into his arms, smiling down at her. "The gun's just for show," he reminded her. "Hagen would think I was crazy if I weren't armed."

"I know that."

His smiled widened. "I love you too."

Katrina sighed a little. "You're just so reckless. Can I help it if I worry about you?"

"Mmmm. Maybe we'd better talk about that. I don't exactly have a risk-free job, sweetheart."

She forced her voice to remain steady. "I know."

He waited, gravely watching her.

A little fiercely she said, "I don't have any right to ask you."

Skye's eyes narrowed. "Then I'll ask you. I don't mind my wife being a hotel manager, but I sure as hell don't want her to be an agent."

"I'm not your wife," she said in a small voice.

"Oh, but you are, sweetheart."

Katrina stared at him. "You divorced me."

He looked a bit sheepish, but his eyes were alight. "Well, no. I set the legal wheels in motion, but I never went through with it. We're still married."

She tried to push him away. "And you never *told* me all this time?"

He kissed her until she didn't have the breath to rail at him, then said, "I love you. I loved you too much then to cut the last tie between us. And I want to marry you again, Trina." His face softened. "Will you marry me, sweetheart?"

"Yes." A few moments later she added uncertainly, "You should have told me, though. I wasn't sure if you wanted a future with me."

"I want a long and settled future with you," he told her in a definite voice. "So I'll retire as an agent if you will."

Katrina searched his eyes. "Are you sure, Skye? If you gave up something you loved because of me—"

He shook his head, smiling. "Ten years is a long time, and I'm tired of the dark. Dane and I are both ready to quit, I think."

She swallowed hard. "What would you do?"

"There's a ranch in Montana I've had my eye on. It's a wild place; it'll need a lot of work." Skye was watching her intently.

Katrina pulled his head down so she could kiss him. "It sounds wonderful. I love you. . . ."

His arm tightened around her, and his eyes were luminous. A bit roughly he said, "I'll probably be a hell of a husband, sweetheart, but they'll put me in the ground before I stop loving you. Don't ever forget that."

Chuckling, she said, "If I've learned anything, it's that I should always wait a few hours after you've said something in a temper, and then ask you if you meant it."

He had to laugh. "Well, I'm glad you've learned that."

The sudden peal of the telephone made Katrina say, "Hagen, wondering where you are."

"Yes." Skye released her reluctantly. "It's time to bring down the curtain."

Hagen was feeling marvelously pleased with himself. He hadn't been able to resist preening a bit when he told Daniel that Gigi was going to marry him, and that rival's crestfallen expression had been an ample reward. It never occurred to him, of course, that Daniel had been playing the same game that Gigi had. He invited Daniel to observe the capture of Adrian, and was even more pleased when Gigi decided to watch as well.

He enjoyed an admiring audience when he was being particularly great.

And the operation went off just as he'd planned. Really, he thought, Skye Prescott was a total professional; though his Katrina had accompanied him to the park, she waited with Gigi, and Prescott was calm and cool. He had listened to Hagen's instruction gravely, and had accepted them with respect.

Hagen wondered if perhaps he had been too hasty in deciding to raise racehorses. If he could manage to entice Prescott away from Daniel, and with that promising beginning rebuild his organization into what it had been . . . It wouldn't hurt, he decided, to est the waters with Prescott. One never knew, after ll.

Hagen stood near the Ferris wheel, but at such an ngle that he wouldn't be visible to a watcher on the un house roof. He looked around, absently taking ote of the costumed employees; there seemed to be nore of them than usual, and he thought indulently that they no doubt wanted a glimpse of the overnor. He consulted his pocket watch, his cupid's ips pursing slightly, then looked at the Ferris wheel.

There had to be an accomplice, of course, or else now could Adrian be certain the governor would be eated in the correct car. He eyed the operator narowly. A young man who looked cheerful and not in he least dangerous. But then, how many of them eally looked dangerous?

Prescott had already disappeared around the fun nouse, and Hagen checked his watch again. The overnor, he decided, should be coming into the ark about now. He looked in the right direction and, within minutes, saw a man in a dark suit surrounded by unobtrusive bodyguards; the crowd milling about hardly noticed.

Hagen looked back at his watch until the sweep hand touched a number, then snapped it closed and returned it to the pocket of his vest. And, right on schedule, he saw Prescott coming back around the un house with one hand on the shoulder of the man n front of him. The man's hands were behind his back, and he looked subdued.

Strolling toward them, Hagen studied Adrian cu-iously. So, he thought, the sketches had been right. A big man, over six feet, with prematurely silver nair. A very big man, in fact, as large as Prescott. In act—Hagen stopped abruptly as the two men approached, and he had the uncertain sensation of the earth shifting beneath his feet.

But that was nonsense. Firmly he said, "Luther Adrian, I hereby arrest you for the crimes of international terrorism." He blinked, staring at his captured killer. In a totally different voice he said, "What the hell—"

"He really doesn't look much like Adrian," a cheerful voice said from off to the right. "It's just a wig, you know, and makeup."

Hagen turned his head slowly and stared. There were two clowns with unpainted faces. He knew those faces. Josh Long held a whirring video camera on one shoulder, and Raven had spoken. Still completely blank, Hagen looked back at his captured killer. Skye Prescott was standing beside him with his arms folded and a smile of unholy amusement on his face—and the killer, whose hands were clearly unbound, was taking off his silver hair. The killer, Hagen realized, looked an awful lot like Skye Prescott.

"This damned wig itches like hell," he complained. He sounded like Prescott, too, but he drawled. He looked at Hagen and said helpfully, "I'm not Adrian."

Hagen found breath. "The governor—"

"The governor isn't here either," Josh Long told him, video camera still whirling. "The gentleman you took to be the governor is one of the hotel waiters. His bodyguards were busboys."

"The bomb—" Hagen tried again.

"Modeling clay," Skye Prescott told him gently. "You should have gotten an analysis, Hagen. That was careless of you."

Raven strolled toward him, smiling. "What you don't seem to understand, maestro, is that you've been royally conned. Luther Adrian was never here. In fact, a couple of Daniel's men have him in cus tody some miles from here. With a little help from us, Skye tracked him down weeks ago."

Hagen had totally lost command of the situation, but he wasn't about to accept it. With a fine show of rage, he roared, "How dare you people interfere with a federal operation."

"Pretty when he's angry, isn't he?" a new voice commented with satisfaction.

Hagen turned his head slowly. They were all there, he realized. All of them. They had been practically under his nose for two weeks, all wearing costumes. There was Rafferty Lewis, and Zach Steele, the one who had just spoken, and Lucas Kendrick—all accompanied by their smiling wives. There was Kelsey. And Derek Ross, with a petite brunette who was clearly his wife. Hagen looked back at the two standing before him, and the bogus Adrian spoke.

"Twins," he murmured. "In fact, you've been calling me Skye for the past week. But I'm Dane." He slipped an arm around the giggling blonde dressed as a chorus dancer who had come out of nowhere to join him. "This is Jenny. My wife."

"I hope you two are quitting," Daniel said severely as he, Gigi, and Katrina joined the group. "You've blown your cover."

Skye pulled Katrina into his arms. "We are." He looked at Hagen with bright eyes. "You know Katrina, of course," he said. "She's my wife."

Gigi grinned. "Is she? I must admit, I wondered about that."

Hagen glared at her. "You *knew* about this?"

"Of course I did," Gigi told him calmly.

Hagen tended to respect deviousness, but he still wasn't prepared to go down without a fight. "You've stabbed me in the back," he raged at her.

"You have used that line before," she observed musingly.

What Hagen might have said to that, they were destined never to know. A sudden awareness made him turn his head slowly and stare at Josh Long. "You're taping this," he said in a hollow voice of realization.

"Naturally." Raven waited until her husband had turned off the camera and lowered it to his side, then said to Hagen, "I read somewhere that a former director of the FBI kept secret tapes and files in case he needed weapons against possible enemies." She smiled. "Daniel isn't that ruthless. So we'll hold the tape, just to make sure you stop using people like pawns."

For the first time, Hagen realized that Raven knew what he had planned to do. He cleared his throat and shot an accusing look at Daniel, but that distinguished gentleman shook his head.

"No, they didn't find out from me. Once they knew, I just confirmed it. You went too far when you tried to kidnap Long to try to persuade his friends to find Adrian for you."

"Much, much too far," Raven said sweetly. "Try anything like that again, and we'll hear of it. You know we will. And we'll release our tape to the media."

"Blackmail!" Hagen said bitterly.

Josh looked at his wife with an expression of mild surprise. "How about that? He understands the concept."

Hagen drew the shreds of his dignity around him and took half a dozen steps away from them. Then he stopped and turned back around, staring at Gigi. "Well?" he snapped.

She was standing with her hands linked before

her, her expression serene. "Well what, John?" she asked gently.

"Are you coming with me?"

She sighed soulfully. "You still want me?"

His eyes narrowed. "Gigi," he began awfully.

Gigi chuckled and went to him. Slipping her hand into the crook of his arm, she said consolingly, "Never mind. We'll raise horses, and you shall enjoy yourself planning strategy for the races."

He led her away, and it was only when they were out of earshot that he said judiciously, "They did that very well. It's a pity they have so many scruples."

She smiled at him. "Yes, John. It certainly is."

Raven looked up at her husband. "John?"

"It does seem a prosaic name for someone like Hagen," Josh agreed dryly.

A gleam entered Raven's eyes. "And speaking of names." She took his hand and they joined the others, who were gathered in a loose group near the fun house. "Kelsey?"

Kelsey took one look at his ex-partner and decided he didn't like the expression in her eyes. "What?" he said warily.

"Your other name," she said gently.

He glanced around to find everyone watching and waiting, curiosity on every face. Looking back at Raven, he half closed his eyes and muttered, "I suppose if I don't tell you, that high-handed husband of yours will dig out my birth certificate."

"We've been very patient," Josh told him.

Kelsey, realizing there was no escape, drew a deep breath and said imploringly, "Look, Elizabeth didn't even know she'd be Mrs. Kelsey until we signed the certificate!"

Raven's expression was stern. "Give!"

Kelsey, who was wearing the garb of a Mississippi riverboat captain, shoved his hat back on his rusty colored hair and glared at her. But, after a moment he said explosively, "It's Tristan!"

Losing control of her expression, Raven exclaimed "Tristan . . ."

Somewhat desperately Kelsey said, "He was a knight at King Arthur's Round Table."

The others lost control then, but it was Teddy who found the perfect comment. Delightedly she exclaimed, "A dragon slayer!"

Epilogue

Just over a year later, Raven Long stood at the bedroom window of a secluded country house in New York State and gazed out on the moonlit night. She was waiting for her husband, who was down the hall persuading their five-month-old son it was time to sleep. It was a nightly ritual, and Josh was convinced that it was because their black-haired, bright-eyed son had somehow discovered that his name—Devlin—meant "fierce valor."

Kelsey had suggested that the child was just mishearing his name, that was all. He heard "devil." Raven had told him he was a fine one to talk of names, and Kelsey had grinned at her.

Raven was feeling content. She hadn't really known contentment until she had met Josh, but these last few years had convinced her it wasn't an illusion. She was her husband's partner and best friend as well as wife and lover, and her life was wonderfully complete.

"He'll rule the world one day," Josh said suddenly

as he came up behind her and slipped his arms around her. "And God help the world."

She laughed. "And you want another one," she teased.

Somewhat wistfully Josh said, "I'd like a girl."

Raven turned in his embrace to smile up at him. "Yes, I know. If Maggie and Rebecca were the daughters of anyone but Zach, you probably would have kidnapped them."

"Maybe it's just something about twins," he mused.

Raven laughed again. "Do you realize we're in the middle of our own baby boom? There must have been a weird alignment of the planets or something."

"Or something," Josh said with a grin.

"Think about it," she insisted. "Rafferty and Sarah already had Patrick, but in the last year, every one of us has become parents. Kelsey and Elizabeth had Steven just a few weeks after we got revenge on the maestro. Then Teddy had the twins, we had Devlin, and not a month later Luc and Kyle had Victoria. Derek and Shannon had Amanda two months ago—"

"And three weeks ago," Josh finished, "Jenny and Katrina both gave birth within an hour of each other."

Raven giggled. "I'll bet the hospital was going nuts. If Skye and Katrina hadn't been visiting Belle Retour because their house was in a shambles from the remodeling . . . You have to admit, the timing was perfect. The oddest thing of all is that although Dane and Jenny had planned Nicholas, Katrina swears she was on the pill when Adam was conceived. She says it was just *like* Skye to get her pregnant despite modern science."

"Reminds me of the old joke," Josh said.

"About the baby being born with a smile on his face and a pill clutched in one hand?" Raven smiled at him, then cleared her throat. "Speaking of which—

our genes appear to produce determined offspring, darling. We'd better name this one Alexandra; she can defend the world from her brother."

Josh blinked. After a moment he said cautiously, "Caviar again?"

"No." Raven looked bemused. "Licorice."

Some time later, having been carried to bed by her adored and adoring husband, Raven said thoughtfully, "Definitely a weird alignment of the planets."

"Or something," Josh agreed tenderly, holding his wife close.

THE EDITOR'S CORNER

Next month we celebrate our sixth year of publishing LOVESWEPT. Behind the scenes, the original team still works on the line with undiminished enthusiasm and pride. Susann is a full editor now, Nita is still the "fastest reader in the East or West," Barbara has written every single piece of back-cover copy (except the three I wrote in the first month, only proving Barbara should do them all), and from afar Elizabeth still edits one or two books each month. And I believe I can safely say that our authors' creative contributions and continuing loyalty to the line is unparalleled. From book #1 (**HEAVEN'S PRICE** by Sandra Brown) to book #329 (next month's **WAITING FOR LILA** by Billie Green) and on into the future, our authors consistently give us their best work and earn our respect and affection more each day.

Now, onward and upward for at least six more great years, here are some wonderful LOVESWEPT birthday presents for you. Joan Elliott Pickart leads off with **TO FIRST BE FRIENDS**, LOVESWEPT #324. Shep Templeton was alive! The award-winning journalist, the only man Emily Templeton had ever loved, hadn't died in the Pataguam jungle, but was coming home—only to learn his wife had divorced him. Eight months before, after a night of reckless passion, he had left for his dangerous assignment. She'd vowed then it was the last time Shep would leave her. Love for Emily was all that had kept Shep going, had made him want to live through months of pain and recovery. Now he had to fight for a new start. . . . Remember, this marvelous book is also available in a beautiful hardcover collector's edition from Doubleday.

In **BOUND TO HAPPEN**, LOVESWEPT #325, by Mary Kay McComas, a breathtaking angel drives Joe Bonner off the road, calls him a trespasser, then faints dead away in his arms. Leslie Rothe had run away from her sister's wedding in confusion, wondering if she'd ever fall

(continued)

in love—or if she even wanted to. Joe awakened turbulent emotions, teased her unmercifully, then kissed her breathless, and taught a worldly woman with an innocent heart how it felt to love a man. But could she prove how much she treasured Joe before her folly destroyed their love?

Next, we introduce an incredibly wonderful treat to you. Deborah Smith begins her Cherokee Trilogy with **SUNDANCE AND THE PRINCESS,** LOVESWEPT #325. (The second romance in the trilogy, **TEMPTING THE WOLF,** will be on sale in June; the final love story, **KAT'S TALE,** will be on sale in August.) In **SUNDANCE AND THE PRINCESS** Jeopard Surprise is Robert Redford gorgeous, a golden-haired outlaw whose enigmatic elegance enthralls Tess Gallatin, makes her want to break all the rules—and lose herself in his arms! He'd come aboard her boat pretending to court the blue-eyed Cherokee princess, but his true mission—to search for a stolen diamond—was endangered by Tess's sweet, seductive laugh. Tess could deny Jep nothing, not her deepest secrets or her mother's precious remembrance, but she never suspected her lover might betray her . . . or imagined how fierce his fury might blaze. An incandescent love story, not to be missed.

LOST IN THE WILD, LOVESWEPT #327, by Gail Douglas, features impossibly gorgeous Nick Corcoran, whose mesmerizing eyes make Tracy Carlisle shiver with desire. But her shyness around her grandfather's corporate heir apparent infuriates her! For three years Nick had considered her off limits, and besides, he had no intention of romancing the snobbish granddaughter of his powerful boss to win the top job. But when Tracy outsmarted a pair of kidnappers and led him into the forest in a desperate escape plan, Nick was enchanted by this courageous woodswoman who embraced danger and risked her life to save his. But could Tracy persuade Nick that by choice she wasn't his rival, only his prize?

(continued)

Peggy Webb gives us pure dynamite in **ANY THURS-DAY**, LOVESWEPT #328. Hannah Donovan is a sexy wildcat of a woman, Jim Roman decided as she pointed her rifle at his chest—definitely a quarry worthy of his hunt! With a devilish, devastating smile, the rugged columnist began his conquest of this beautiful Annie Oakley by kissing her with expert, knowing lips . . . and Hannah felt wicked, wanton passion brand her cool scientist's heart. Jim wore power and danger like a cloak, challenged and intrigued her as few men ever had—but she had to show him she couldn't be tamed . . . or possessed. Could they stop fighting destiny and each other long enough to bridge their separate worlds? A fabulous romance!

Remember Dr. Delilah Jones? In **WAITING FOR LILA**, LOVESWEPT #329, Billie Green returns to her characters of old for a raucous good time. Lila had special plans for the medical conference in Acapulco—this trip she was determined to bag a husband! She enlisted her best friends as matchmakers, invited them to produce the perfect candidate—rich, handsome, successful—then spotted the irresistibly virile man of her dreams all by herself. Bill Shelley was moonstruck by the elegant lady with the voice like raw silk, captivated by this mysterious, seductive angel who seemed to have been made just for him. Once he knew her secrets, could Bill convince her that nothing would keep her as safe and happy as his enduring love? A pure delight from Billie!

Enjoy!

Carolyn Nichols

Carolyn Nichols
Editor
LOVESWEPT
Bantam Books
666 Fifth Avenue
New York, NY 10103

BANTAM NEVER SOUNDED SO GOOD
NEW SUBLIMINAL SELF-HELP TAPES
FROM BANTAM AUDIO PUBLISHING
Invest in the powers of your mind.

Years of extensive research and personal experience have proved that it is possible to release powers hidden in the subconscious through the rise of subliminal suggestion. Now the Bantam Audio Self-Help series, produced by Audio Activation, combines sophisticated psychological techniques of behavior modification with subliminal stimulation that will help you get what you want out of life.

☐ 45106	GET A GOOD NIGHT'S SLEEP . . . EVERY NIGHT: FEMALE	$7.95
☐ 45107	GET A GOOD NIGHT'S SLEEP . . . EVERY NIGHT: MALE	$7.95
☐ 45041	STRESS-FREE FOREVER: FEMALE	$7.95
☐ 45042	STRESS-FREE FOREVER: MALE	$7.95
☐ 45081	YOU'RE IRRESISTIBLE!: FEMALE	$7.95
☐ 45082	YOU'RE IRRESISTIBLE!: MALE	$7.95
☐ 45004	SLIM FOREVER: FOR WOMEN	$7.95
☐ 45005	SLIM FOREVER: FOR MEN	$7.95
☐ 45022	POSITIVELY CHANGE YOUR LIFE: FOR WOMEN	$7.95
☐ 45023	POSITIVELY CHANGE YOUR LIFE: FOR MEN	$7.95
☐ 45035	STOP SMOKING FOREVER: FOR WOMEN	$7.95
☐ 45036	STOP SMOKING FOREVER: FOR MEN	$7.95
☐ 45094	IMPROVE YOUR CONCENTRATION: WOMEN	$7.95
☐ 45095	IMPROVE YOUR CONCENTRATION: MEN	$7.95
☐ 45112	AWAKEN YOUR SENSUALITY: FEMALE	$7.95
☐ 45113	AWKAEN YOUR SENSUALITY: MALE	$7.95
☐ 45130	DEVELOP INTUITION: WOMEN	$7.95
☐ 45131	DEVELOP INTUITION: MEN	$7.95
☐ 45016	PLAY TO WIN: WOMEN	$7.95
☐ 45017	PLAY TO WIN: MEN	$7.95
☐ 45010	WEALTH, COME TO YOU: FEMALE	$7.95
☐ 45011	WEALTH, COME TO YOU: MALE	$7.95

Look for them at your local bookstore, or use this handy page to order.

- -

NEW!

Handsome Book Covers Specially Designed To Fit Loveswept Books

Our new French Calf Vinyl book covers come in a set of three great colors— royal blue, scarlet red and kachina green.

Each 7" × 9½" book cover has two deep vertical pockets, a handy sewn-in bookmark, and is soil and scratch resistant.

To order your set, use the form below.